THE LE(

SERIES TITLES

The Clayfields
Elise Gregory

Kind of Blue
Christopher Chambers

Evangelina Everyday
Dawn Burns

Township
Jamie Lyn Smith

Responsible Adults
Patricia Ann McNair

Great Escapes from Detroit
Joseph O'Malley

Nothing to Lose
Kim Suhr

The Appointed Hour
Susanne Davis

"This magnificent collection should be savored around a campfire or under the covers on a cold night. Wildfires, plummeting helicopters, and unforgiving wilderness confront these characters, as they struggle with love and relationships. The author pairs his deep knowledge of working in the woods and life in the West with compassion for the human condition. *Greyhound Cowboy* is a thrilling and satisfying read."

—MICHAEL FREED-THALL
author of *Horodno Burning*

GREYHOUND COWBOY

AND OTHER STORIES

KEN POST

CORNERSTONE PRESS
UNIVERSITY OF WISCONSIN-STEVENS POINT

Cornerstone Press, Stevens Point, Wisconsin 54481
Copyright © 2024 Ken Post
www.uwsp.edu/cornerstone

Printed in the United States of America by
Point Print and Design Studio, Stevens Point, Wisconsin

Library of Congress Control Number: 2024914677
ISBN: 978-1-960329-39-4

Cover art by Jessy Post.

Cornerstone Press titles are produced in courses and internships offered by the
Department of English at the University of Wisconsin–Stevens Point.

DIRECTOR & PUBLISHER
Dr. Ross K. Tangedal

EXECUTIVE EDITORS
Jeff Snowbarger, Freesia McKee

EDITORIAL DIRECTOR
Ellie Atkinson

SENIOR EDITORS
Brett Hill, Grace Dahl

PRESS STAFF
Paige Biever, Carolyn Czerwinski, Sophie McPherson, Eva Nielsen, Natalie Reiter,
Angelina Sherman, Ava Willett

For Anne

STORIES

THE LOOKOUT

Holt finished taking weather observations, wrote them in the logbook, and noted the date and time: June 29, 1974, 12:30 p.m. Twelve volumes of logbooks spanning three decades of general observations, lonely musings, and ruminations on life and love provided engaging reading. Some real characters inhabited this Forest Service lookout planted 8,267 feet above sea level. He started to nod off in the warmth and lay on the thin muslin-covered mattress to take a nap. The summer in the lookout was clearing the cobwebs that had accumulated in his life.

Holt sunk into a serene slumber when a faint, "Helloooo? Anybody up there?" floated up to him. At first, he thought it was a dream, but discerned it was a person calling from the base of the tower. He heard footsteps ascending, and by the time Holt was up and moving to the door, a young woman wearing a sweaty T-shirt and cutoff jeans had opened the trap door in the catwalk.

"Hi, I'm Morningstar, but you can call me Star." She put her hand out to shake.

Holt was surprised to see anyone after three weeks, especially eleven miles from the road. Groggy from the nap, he grasped her hand half-heartedly. "Nice to meet you, Star."

Star lifted an enormous olive colored Kelty backpack off and set it on the catwalk, where it leaned against the guardrail surrounding the lookout.

"Wow, you are really on some kind of expedition." Holt struggled to lift it with one hand. "How much does that darn thing weigh?" He looked at Star, thin with straight sandy-blonde hair and a slight gap in her front teeth. She was busy rubbing a red spot on her shoulder where the pack strap tattooed her. A few beads of sweat on her forehead cleared a path through the trail grime, giving her a faint striped look.

"My trek is over. This is the end of the road for me." Star gave him a broad grin.

Holt half-squinted at her, as if he hadn't heard her correctly or didn't grasp the meaning of her words, and chalked it up to his sleepiness wearing off. "After that long hike, would you like to come inside?"

Holt handed Star a glass of powdered lemonade.

"Thank you very much. You know, you never told me your name."

"Sorry, it's Holt."

"It's a nice name." Star wiped her mouth with the back of her hand and set the glass down on top of the small propane refrigerator. "Bartender, can I get another?"

"I'll have to mix one up."

"I'm in no hurry."

With his back toward Star, Holt pulled a jug of cold water from the fridge, poured in the powder, and stirred it with a spoon. There was something about Star and her arrival Holt could not decipher. "So, are you going to head back down the trail, or are you planning to bushwhack into the next valley?" He handed her the glass and sat down.

"Actually, I'm going to bide my time, and enjoy this mountaintop for a while. It's so beautiful up here." Star stepped toward the windows, looking away from Holt and out at the expanse of mountains rolling away in all directions. "This place is unbelievable. I appreciate you sharing it with me."

"No problem with the sharing part. Besides, it doesn't belong to me. The Forest Service owns it."

"You're kind of like the owner."

"I look at it more like I'm a caretaker."

Star lifted the glass to him in a salute. "Okay. Can I ask you a favor?"

"Sure."

"Can I stay here with you?"

Holt stood up as if he sat on a tack. "You mean today?"

"No," Star looked at Holt, "I mean stay here."

Holt stammered, "I don't think the Forest Service will allow that. I'm the lookout they hired." He moved away and fiddled with the rotating ring of the Osborne range-finder hoping to deflect the question. *Where exactly was this going?* A woman shows up at his lookout and unabashedly decides she wants to encamp there. There was nothing in the Forest Service paperwork about how to deal with a situation like this, probably because it never happened before. Holt didn't normally care one way or another about rules; like anyone else, he favored the ones which worked to his advantage and frowned on those that didn't. Her request was probably crossing a line. He repeated: "I don't think it's allowed." There—that should do it. He made himself pretty clear on the government's position.

"I wasn't asking if the Forest Service was okay with it." Star circled around to the other side of the rangefinder and put her hand on the ring so Holt couldn't move it. "I was asking if you were okay with it. There's a difference."

A gentle thrumming flared in Holt's head. One minute he's alone in a lookout, miles from anywhere. The next minute he's a got a perfect stranger asking to share his 14 by 14-foot lookout for an indefinite period. Sure, she was female, and not bad-looking, but it was more than Holt was able to process in the short course of their conversation.

Star seemed to be reading his mind. "Who's gonna know, anyway? It's only the two of us up here. I doubt whether the government is going to be all worked up I'm here. I'm not some kind of saboteur or anything. I'm minding my own business."

"Here's the thing," Holt stalled, trying to make her understand or to help him grasp what was going on. "It's kind of an unusual request and I'm trying to sort out what it is you want or are looking for."

"I should start over because I can see why you think it's a bit out of the ordinary." Star maneuvered around the rangefinder further and got within an arm's reach of Holt. "It was a vision—this is the place I need to be. It's the right time to be on a mountaintop—this mountaintop. I was camping and saw a light at night way up the valley and I feel like a moth drawn to it. I can't explain it any more than a moth knows why it is attracted. Something spoke to me about it and I can't help you were here first."

There was silence as Holt parsed her logic and his comfort level. Instead of leveling off slowly, the mental scale in his head kept clanging up and down. He enjoyed his isolation and doing whatever he wanted, whenever he wanted. Now, the dynamic shifted. At the same time, she was harmless and it would be nice to talk with someone from time to time. The place was pretty small but Holt knew couples were lookouts before because the logbook went back many years containing all their ramblings. Of course, Holt and Star weren't a couple. Where would she sleep? He glanced around the lookout and remembered the folded-up cot in the corner when someone extra needed to stay over. She must have brought her own food because her pack weighed a ton. He settled in to the notion there'd be no harm in it.

"I guess we could try it out on a day-to-day thing. I won't say anything to my boss as long as you don't interfere with my job."

Star put out her hand. "Deal."

They shifted a few things around the lookout and pushed the assembled cot against the opposite wall across from Holt's bed. Star took out a down sleeping bag from her backpack, fluffed it up, and set it on the cot, while Holt made room for her food on the shelves in the tiny kitchen cabinet. Everything else was in five-gallon buckets with lids on them and stashed in various crannies of the lookout. He set her bags of rice, beans, and dried tofu on the shelves. He won't be eating much of her stuff. Not a candy bar in sight.

"I'm going to give you some space for a bit while I do some exploring." Star put on a baseball cap with a big peace sign on the front. On her way out the door she said, "There must be water around here. Want me to get some?"

"Much appreciated. Grab a water jug at the base of the tower. I'm afraid you're going to have to put on the pack frame near the jugs. Lash the full jug to the pack."

Star rubbed her shoulders subconsciously. "No point fussing about it. We're going to need water. How far is it?"

"About a half-mile down the side of the mountain, there's a narrow trail going down opposite the side you came up. It starts right past the outhouse." Holt moved to the side of the tower and pointed it out to Star. "It's actually a small dammed-up spring."

"I think I'm going to soak my feet and wash up—downstream of our drinking water supply." Star put on her hiking boots and *thunk-thunked* down all forty-two steps of the metal stairwell.

Holt watched her meander down the trail, disappearing into a thicket. Without turning her back she waved her hand as if she knew she was watched.

Two hours later, Star returned with the container of water strapped to the pack frame and a five-gallon bucket in her hand. Holt watched her approach in the late afternoon heat. The beauty of life in a lookout was seeing everything. It all unfolded right in front of Holt because he was highest and always observing, even when he wasn't conscious of it. Movement, changes in light, and clouds morphing into objects not noticed in another setting, were enough to give pause and ponder them.

"What should I do with the water?" Star yelled up to the tower.

"Hold on, I'll be right down." Holt scrambled down the stairwell and helped remove the pack from Star's back. "What's in the bucket?"

"It's a surprise. I'll show you later."

"Let me show you what we do with the water." A double pulley system was rigged from the upper part of the tower and the rope hung down to almost ground level where it was tied off to the base of the tower. "No need to haul that up the tower when we have this handy setup right here." He tied the jug to the pulley system and hauled it skyward until it reached the metal arm extending over the tower's catwalk. Holt knotted the rope at the bottom of the tower. "That was easy."

Star looked at the water jug suspended thirty-five feet over her head. "How much can that thing lift?"

"I don't know exactly but it's pretty heavy-duty. I think they hauled up all the building material, propane tanks, and other stuff with it. That metal arm is like an I-beam and it's got at least eight lag bolts in the wall. Don't worry, that jug isn't going to fall on our heads."

They finished eating dinner—lentils for Star and macaroni and cheese for Holt—when Holt remembered the five-gallon bucket Star carried. "What's in the bucket?"

"More food. I set it in the woods below treeline on the way up."

"You mean you hauled a bucket *and* pack eleven miles?"

"I stopped more often because my arms got tired. Switched arms a lot too."

Holt glanced at her arms. They weren't overly muscular, more sinewy than anything. He knew what it took to haul a filled five-gallon bucket uphill for eleven miles. His admiration for Star grew. *My God, she could be here all summer.*

The sun began to go down and Star said, "Let's sit outside and watch the sunset."

"I'm afraid I have only one chair but you can use the bucket to sit on."

"That will work." She stepped out into the cool air. "Oh, I love the way the air feels and smells. Do you smell it?"

Holt wasn't sure what the "it" was, but the air *did* feel good. When the sun went down further, the air turned bracing.

The sun dipped low and parked below the horizon, the valley fading into a deep green. A light breeze's whisper fluttered up the valley before they felt it. She sat on the catwalk, her knees folded to her chest, and Holt in his folding throne next to her. There was no awkwardness in the silence, broken only by an occasional comment or observation as twilight progressed. They were just there. Holt's thoughts strayed in many directions but they all led back to the aura of Star's serenity. It was similar to the calmness his mother possessed; nothing fazed her, and her equanimity touched all. With Star, though, it was deeper, more penetrating. The quiet was freeing, opening a space to think about his mom. He had brought a few of her recipes on four-by-six-inch index cards with him, hoping to make them. Her handwritten notations, "double this, more salt" brought a smile to his face.

Stars were already aglow in the east when Holt said, "I think it's time for bed. I'll see you in the morning." The faint outline of her face was visible, and Holt wondered what tomorrow had in store after the surprises of today.

"Holt," Star paused for a moment, "You're a good caretaker."

Holt was in such a deep sleep his body felt like a day-old cement pour when he finally awakened. He rubbed his eyes and looked around trying to get his bearings. He remembered his company. Holt looked at Star's cot, but all he saw was her powder-blue sleeping bag shoved to the side of it. He took advantage of her absence to quickly throw some clothes on. Holt fumbled with the stove to get the coffee water heating and stepped outside. "Jesus, you scared the shit out of me!"

Star was sitting on the deck of the catwalk out of sight below the window with her hands around her knees and using the wall for a backrest, admiring the scenery. "I didn't want to go back in and wake you since you were sleeping so soundly. Besides, this is my favorite time of day; I saw the sunrise and it started out red, changed to purple and then orange. It's so quiet early in the morning and you can hear all the birds sing."

"You gave me a real shock. I was probably half asleep. I got some water heating up—want some coffee?"

"I'll take the water for my tea. Do you like chamomile?"

"I'm afraid I'm pretty much just a coffee drinker at this hour. Speaking of time, I have to do my morning check-in on the radio in a few minutes."

Star quickly shifted. "Don't say anything about me—you promised."

"My word is good. But don't be making noise in the background when I call in."

For a week Star disappeared into the woods for hours, or sunned herself like a marmot on the big flat rock where the trail dropped out of sight. She came back from her explorations bearing little gifts of pine cones, flowers, feathers, animal bones, or rocks for Holt. "Everything has a story to tell and nothing is too small to appreciate." Star looked at Holt with a smile and handed them to him with reverence and a sense of amazement Holt only saw before in the eyes of children who discover an object for the first time.

"Holt, sometimes you look lost in thought. Is something bothering you?" Star was cooking a cheese and onion quesadilla on the stove, the smell filling their small space.

"I've been thinking about my mom," Holt said. "She passed away a year ago from a brain tumor and I'm working my way through it. Probably will be for a long time, too."

"I'm so sorry," said Star.

Holt wanted to talk about his mom to somebody, but never found the right moment, and it felt like a stone dropping into a deep well. With Star, though, he saw in her eyes, a kindness and yearning to understand his hurt.

Star flipped the quesadilla onto a plate. "It must be terrible to see someone wither away like that. Is that why you're up here—to get away?"

"Pretty much."

* * *

As much as Holt loved his home, his mom's death had darkened a place that used to have so much light. It became too confining as if all the walls were encroaching on his life. The lookout was the perfect solution; expansive views in all directions with sun pouring in from each side.

He found out about the job when his dad saw an ad in the newspaper. Holt had been reading in their living room when his father walked in and handed him a cutout piece of paper.

Holt had studied the page, sensing his father watching him. "So why do you think I want to be a lookout?"

"You seem a bit lost. Sometimes alone time is a good thing." His father placed his hand on Holt's shoulder, with a calm, benevolent look normally associated with a preacher.

"What makes you think that?" Holt knew his father saw right through that response. If Holt wasn't exactly lost, he certainly was adrift. He had lost himself in exertion: cutting and splitting firewood, lung-bursting runs, and endless bench presses in the basement. The rest of life was shunted aside. He took the application from his father.

* * *

Star moved away from the stove and dug into a backpack pocket. She pulled out a whitebark pine cone painted gold. She reached out, took his hand and pressed the pine cone into it, curling each finger around it until his hand closed. "This is a memory cone. This is where all the good memories of your mom are stored. When you are sad, when the grief hits, this cone will bring you back to cherish her."

Holt turned the cone over in his hand, running his fingers over the cone's hard carapace.

"Holt, you're going to have a very good life. When you're done here, I want you to get on with it."

"Thank you. What about you?" Holt looked at Star. "What do you want to do?"

Star gazed off toward the horizon. "I try not to make plans or have hopes or dreams. I want to live for the day I'm in."

On stormy days when rain dotted the windows they read silently, the pages rustling like dried leaves, or drinking tea. Holt discovered chamomile tea wasn't bad. There were days though, when Star inexplicably came into the lookout without saying anything and burrowed into her sleeping bag and lay there motionless. On other days, she never got up except to pee. Holt couldn't tell if she was sleeping or ill, and was unsure what to make of this behavior. He tiptoed around the lookout or gave her space on sunny days by taking a book and reclining against the tower's legs as a backrest.

A second week passed and Star began a ritual of leaving words or phrases for Holt on the little table serving as their kitchen area. One day it was his name spelled out in tiny garnets she dug out of the mountain's slopes. Another time she depicted a sunrise made out of porcupine quills found on her daily expeditions. The best was when she laid a chocolate bar on the table since chocolate was scarce and surrounded it with blueberries. A collection of small rocks said: "A feast."

One night lying awake in his sleeping bag, he grabbed the memory cone. Simple, yet it worked. With cone in hand, he remembered baking cookies with his mom, hearing her cheer from the bleachers at his little league games, and listening to his favorite bedtime Dr. Seuss stories. It was more than a physical gift Star gave him; she was blessed with an ability to see into a person's heart and soothe it.

They had fallen into a rhythm like a married couple: He took temperature, relative humidity, and moisture content measurements from the little white, louvered weather station at the base of the tower. Tromping up four flights of zigzag stairs, he called the data in to the office in Three Forks, and scanned for fires. Star rose early and often

disappeared for hours. One afternoon, Holt chopped firewood, carried it from below tree line, loaded the wood in
a box attached to the pulley system, and walked up the
stairs to unload it, only to find Star drinking her tea. It
was unsettling the way she quietly slipped by him like
clouds wafting over the summit, along with her knack
of blending in and disappearing into the woods, as if
she melted into the landscape. Holt always stumbled and
crashed through things, snapping brush, scuffing rocks,
announcing himself to the forest.

Holt entered a newfound state of contentment. The
world slowed and their mountaintop seemed more alive
with birdsong and the scent of sap flowing in the pines.
There was no way to explain the lack of sexual edge which
normally crept into a man and a woman living together,
particularly in such tight confines. Maybe it was Star's
waif-like appearance, though underneath, he knew she
was tough as horse hide. They saw each other more as
two minds in a 196-square foot building rather than two
bodies. Everything was in balance.

One day, a wall of slate-colored clouds rushed toward them
and trees bent to the wind as bits of arboreal debris flew
past. Lightning streaked, and the detonation of thunder
shook the mountains, vibrating from ridge to ridge. The
lookout shuddered, and its guy wires hummed like over-
strained strings in a hellish symphony. The surge of energy
from the approaching storm fascinated Holt, but he also
sensed his body tensing as if ready to receive a blow.

Star turned to him and said, "This is incredible! It's like
watching some totally cool movie."

Holt didn't answer but noticed the wind slowed considerably. There was a tapping on the roof like pebbles tossed on it. The patter grew louder, and sheets of hail pounded the tin roof with a din, making it hard to hear. Hail bounced off the roof, catwalk, and handrails.

Holt watched in disbelief as Star stepped out of her jeans. "What are you doing?"

"I've always wanted to stand naked in a hail storm. I'm going outside." Star dropped her flannel shirt in the pile with her pants and was ready to take off her underwear and bra, when she turned to Holt. "I don't want you leering at me."

"I'm not leering at you—you're getting undressed right in front of me so it's pretty hard to avoid seeing you."

"Looking is one thing, leering is another."

"Okay, I promise not to leer, though I wasn't doing it."

"Good." Star took off the rest of her clothes and pranced to the door.

Holt looked at her naked body, but tried not to be too obvious. She was thin and white where the sun hadn't tanned her pale skin, and knew she was used to doing physical labor by the set of the muscles.

Star leaned on the catwalk handrail and hail bounced off her head, hands, and uplifted arms. With her head tilted skyward she danced, soaking up everything.

Holt watched, bemused, and bewildered by the spontaneity and lack of modesty, but felt the hair on his arms start to stand up. The hair on the back of his neck tugged his skin. He touched his head and his hair was standing up too. The ring on his finger started making a weird buzzing sound. In two quick steps he was at the door. He grabbed Star, yanking her inside.

"What are you doing?!" she shrieked.

Holt pushed her toward a low stool with glass insulated feet on it and yelled, "Stand on this!" He positioned them on it, arms wrapped around her to keep them stable on a stool made to fit one person. A few seconds afterward, a flash as bright as burning phosphorous filled the lookout with a blazing whiteness that lit up every fiber in their bodies. Instantly, a blast of thunder concussed them, the shock tipped them off, and they fell to the floor in a jumble. They both screamed when the lightning hit but it was drowned out by the thunder. On the floor they gasped like two people who were shoved underwater and suddenly emerged. Star was draped on top of Holt, both realizing how lucky they were to be alive. They lay still until Star burst out laughing.

"Oh man, that was amazing." She couldn't stop laughing.

Holt started laughing too until his diaphragm hurt. They were exhausted although it was only seconds that had transpired, warped in time by the force of the storm's intensity.

"More like amazingly stupid. I should have known better." Holt felt soreness seeping into his back where he landed on it.

"But you were alive, totally alive when it happened." She looked at Holt for a few seconds. "That thread between life and death is so thin. And we were right there. Don't you see?"

"I like the alive part, best. I don't want to find out if lightning will strike twice here." It didn't make sense that a person needed to almost die to feel alive. He had survived his mom passing away, and he didn't want to be any closer to death.

Star pushed herself up with a hand on Holt's chest. "I'm getting cold." She stood up and walked to the pile of clothes and got dressed, not acknowledging her nakedness in front of Holt. He watched and realized he was not leering; he was observing this interesting creature who had landed like some kind of extraterrestrial. One he didn't understand though they were speaking the same language. A feeling of protectiveness came over him, like Star was a sister getting dressed, and he looked away as the waning storm moved toward the next range.

Over the next three days, Holt noticed Star's energy dissipate as if the lightning had sapped her energy. She appeared sullen and frustrated, at one point slamming a book closed after reading a disquieting passage. Holt had seen this languor before, but never so pronounced or prolonged.

"Can I get you some tea?" Holt asked.

"Sure," was Star's only response.

Her effervescence was gone and it was hard to understand Star's pendulum swings so Holt figured he'd wait until her spark returned, and tried to give her more space. He painted the outhouse, rigged a new clothesline, and shored-up the leaky dam where they got their drinking water.

On the fourth day since the storm, morning sun slanted into the lookout as Holt lay in bed. He felt uneasy although there was no palpable reason on such a nice morning. He half sat up in his bed and saw Star was gone, but that was not unusual given her crepuscular wanderings. The sense that something was not right pushed him from his warm bed and he hurried to dress from the clothes in a pile on the floor. The air warmed as he walked to the sunny side of the catwalk near the rope pulley. He didn't notice it at first but the normally slack rope was taut. He went over to it and his eyes followed the line down to the ground.

At the end of it was Star's suspended body.

Holt grabbed the handrail and leaned so far over it straining to see better, he almost fell out of the tower. With a burst of energy, he flew around the catwalk, flipped open the trap door and clambered down the steps two at a time.

The folding chair and a whole round of firewood were askew below her. Holt determined she had rigged a scaffold and kicked them over. Star hung limp like a jacket on a coat hook. Holt climbed onto the chair to try and release her body from the strain on the knot by lifting her. A skein of drool clung to her chin and a red furrow cut into her throat.

He knew lifting wasn't going to work with the rope around her neck. He yelled "Shit!" so loud it reverberated around the mountaintop.

Every passing second was crucial and Holt charged up the stairs, grabbed his pocketknife and ran back down. He slashed at the rope, watching each strand sever until she was suddenly released. The rapid loss of tension catapulted Holt and Star off the chair, and he landed on top of her. He ripped the remnants of the noose off her neck.

"Star! Star! Speak to me, goddammit!" Holt smacked her cheeks and held his head to her nose and chest to search for any sign of breathing. Nothing. He frantically tried to remember his CPR training and began giving chest compressions and rescue breathing. There was no way he could bear to look at Star so he shut his eyes and blocked out all thought except arms pumping and counting. Pressing harder, ribs cracked. A dullness set into his muscles, his knees ached, and the effort turned into a mental fog where thoughts collided and stars appeared before his eyes. It was a warm wetness on his hand before Holt realized he was crying.

The sun continued its ascent and Holt was vaguely aware of how long he was pumping by the increasing warmth of the morning. No sign of life. His body gave out and he slumped prone on his knees. He noiselessly tipped over and lay on his back in the morning dew with the sun beaming on his face.

Movement was painful but necessary. He clumped up the stairs, retrieved Star's sleeping bag, staggered down the steps holding on to the rail so he didn't pitch over. Shaking out the bag, he placed it over Star's body and headed back up the tower.

Holt stood with the radio microphone in his hand trying to figure out what he was going to say. The last thing he wanted to do was talk. He put the mic up to his mouth and his arm dropped to his side, the mic dangling by its pigtail cord down by his knee. At another time he might be embarrassed or ashamed for letting Star stay with him when she wasn't supposed to be there, but none of those feelings mattered now. The glare from the sun shifted, illuminating Holt on the glass in front of him. A belea- guered, expressionless ghost stared back. Numb, depleted, a carcass picked clean. He picked up the mic again and pressed the button to talk.

An hour later, a helicopter's rotors reverberated off the walls of the mountains, and it rose toward the lookout like a hawk riding a thermal. It landed fifty yards from the lookout, the pilot shut down the engine, and Holt saw three people climb out: a state trooper in uniform with the dark piping on his trousers clearly visible, the district ranger, and a third person he didn't recognize. Holt sat at the base of the lookout, not far from Star's body.

The district ranger was thin and weathered as a lodgepole fence rail with gray, close-cropped hair, and skin creased by years in the field. "You okay, son?"

Holt turned a red face streaked by tears to the ranger and answered, "No, no I'm not okay."

The trooper started taking pictures from different vantage points while the other man pulled the sleeping bag off Star's body and examined the marks on her neck. The trooper referred to the man as 'Doc,' so Holt figured he must be a physician.

"Why don't we go in the lookout and catch up while these folks get on with their business," the ranger said, tilting his head toward Doc and the trooper.

It was an effort to stand up. His body was one immense sandbag. The climb up the lookout seemed to take an hour, and at one point, Holt braced himself against a railing before moving on. At the lookout, he fell onto his bed, staring up at the roof while the ranger unfolded the chair. Fifteen minutes later, the trooper and doctor climbed the stairs and were in the lookout, which suddenly was crowded and suffocatingly hot. Everyone else was warm too because the ranger got up and opened two windows. Revived enough, Holt's story unspooled while the trooper scribbled notes on a small pad, clicking his pen when another question came to him.

"I'll stay here with the body and the chopper can return for us later." The trooper put the pen and pad in his shirt chest pocket and snapped the flap.

The body. It all sounded so detached. This was no *body*; it was Star. She was a living, breathing person a few hours ago.

Holt buckled his seatbelt and they flew from the lookout in the helicopter. As they coasted down the valley, Holt replayed the last few weeks over in his mind, frame-by-frame, like an old movie reel. He hoped to see some tell-tale hint of why Star killed herself or why she needed a mountaintop to do it. It didn't make sense—nothing made sense anymore. If Star planned this whole thing, he was as much a victim as anyone else. He was the one who cut her body down, poured every drop of sweat inside him into CPR, and held her lifeless body in his arms.

Holt sat at an office desk and completed his termination paperwork. Fired. Kaput. It seemed only yesterday he got hired, filled with the anticipation of spending a summer in the woods to help blot his grief.

The ranger stepped into the room, coffee cup in hand. "Grab any gear you have in the bunkhouse and be back here in fifteen minutes."

Holt packed the rest of the gear he had stowed in a bunkhouse locker, and crossed the parking lot to the ranger station with two weathered army duffle bags. The ranger was waiting for him, leaning against a porch rail.

"Looks like I'm going to be heading up to Missoula tomorrow. They want to talk with me about this, uh—'event.'"

Holt shifted uncomfortably but met the ranger's blue eyes, trying to divine what was happening.

"This has caused a ruckus from here to Missoula." The ranger unscrewed his thermos, poured coffee into the cup, and took a gulp. "The agency doesn't like black eyes. I figure I'm in for a good ass-chewing over this."

"None of this is your fault."

A few seconds ticked by and Holt scanned his face quickly, straining for an interpretation in the ranger's silence. It came to him; shit and water flow downhill and big dominos knock over small dominos. The ranger was in for an official thrashing and Holt was fired. He felt like the smallest domino on the face of the earth.

"Not sure they'll see it the same way. Anyway, the troopers called and they said they don't need any more information from you. If they do, they know how to find you." The ranger tossed the rest of his coffee in the dirt. "You're free to go. Best to put all this behind us and head out now." No handshake was extended, and he met the ranger's sharp gaze. The ranger nodded almost imperceptibly as if to say, *hit the road.*

Holt tossed the duffle bags into the bed of his truck and sped from the parking lot. A cloud of dust hung in the rearview mirror. Soon he was navigating the curves of the two-lane, holding his hand to his eyes to shade them from the sunlight. It flickered *light-dark, light-dark* through the trees. The road opened up and passed meadows brimming with wild flowers, cut by clear creeks flowing through them. Vistas of the mountains appeared, some craggy and rock-covered, others topped by green on the cloudless morning.

Reaching for a stick of Wrigley gum in his jacket pocket, he felt another item. The memory cone. His palm closed on it, holding it firmly as if a special energy passed to him. Overcome, he pulled to the side of the road where he wept so violently, he accidentally hit the horn—a shriek echoing up the valley—and startled himself. Events crowded in: Star handing him the memory cone, and baking holiday cookies with his mom. Holt wiped his eyes and nose on the jacket sleeve, and sat back in his seat for a few minutes before pulling back on the road. He set the cone on the dashboard above the steering wheel, like a compass guiding him.

Around one turn he saw it—his lookout—a speck at this distance but it loomed like a tombstone in his mind. He imagined an epitaph but it was more of a message from Star: "You have a good life, get on with it." It was hard to comprehend how the darkness of Star's mind conquered the lightness of her heart. Two deaths in a little over a year: his mom and Star. Both hurt, but in different ways. He didn't want to be defined or shaped by death; he was too young for that. He was alive, whether it was by luck or fate, and he wanted to make the most of it. The truck entered a long straight section of road and the sun blazed directly on the blacktop. He wanted to run toward life instead of running away. Holt pushed down on the accelerator, felt the truck surge and said, "Get on with it," as the valley disappeared behind him.

GREYHOUND COWBOY

The snowstorm hit with such ferocity the interstate between Bozeman and Billings lay obliterated in heaving sheets of snow. The Greyhound passed a tipped-over semi, cars angled in ditches, and pickup trucks 360-ed into the drifts. Reaching Billings at 10:00 p.m., the bus rolled into a white-washed ghost town.

In the Greyhound terminal, Kurt watched the driver cut the engine. The driver, thick in the chest with a crew cut, stood at the front of the bus. "Listen up, everyone," he folded his arms over his chest. "Roads are all shut down, nothing's open, and our scheduled departure in one hour isn't happening." Pausing to look at his sore-backed, weary passengers, the driver said, "You can sleep on the bus but there's no heat, or you can stay in the terminal where it's warm. Your choice. One more thing: you can grab your luggage now if you want. We'll reload when the roads clear."

The bus door hissed open and Kurt and eight other passengers staggered into the dim confines of the loading area. The driver opened the bus's cargo bay. Passengers milled about while the driver crawled to retrieve the luggage that had slid to the back. Out came an Air Force duffle bag for the scrawny uniformed kid with zits who said, "Thank you, sir." A young mother with a curly-haired boy around four years old waited for the suitcases the driver handed them. A leather saddle materialized and Kurt figured it belonged to the lean guy who had been sitting a seat in front of him, on the other side of the aisle. A weather-beaten cowboy hat cocked over his head while he snored. Kurt's backpack and a long plastic tube carrying his precious custom-made fly rods slid over to him. Some people carried a family Bible, Kurt never went anywhere without the rods, even if he wasn't planning on wetting a line.

Everybody filed into the terminal and the driver followed them. He looked at Kurt and the cowboy. "You fellas good for now?"

"I'll make do."

"No worries here," said the cowboy.

"Good. I'm gonna try to get some sleep on the back seat of the bus." He pulled his big Greyhound parka around him and zipped it. "If something comes up, you know where to find me."

"Sure thing," said Kurt. He dropped his pack and rod case on the floor and picked up a rumpled copy of the Billings Gazette somebody left on a seat. Nothing on the front page caught his eye so he walked to the double doors of the terminal entrance. Outside, in the muted glow of the streetlights and neon signs, snow piled up in storefront doorways. Skeins of snow whisked by the wind sparkled in their passing. Kurt wasn't even halfway to his destination of Minneapolis to see Laura, his girlfriend and PhD candidate. The trip was a whirl of mixed emotions. The last visit vacillated between stony silence over Kurt's comment to her about scientific esoterica and uproarious stoned potlucks with her fellow students. Maybe this blizzard was an omen.

"Some storm, huh?" said the cowboy.

Mesmerized by the blowing snow, Kurt hadn't noticed the cowboy standing next to him. "Yeah." He kept facing the window. "Wonder when it'll end."

"No telling."

They turned to look at one another for the first time. Kurt saw an older guy, late forties with short, blond hair under his hat, and eyes as blue and clear as the pools stacked with trout on the Beaverhead River. He was creased from a scorching sun and scoured by cruel winds.

"I should make a call," Kurt said.

"Good luck." The cowboy pointed to the payphone with the phone receiver ripped from its cable.

"I'll use my cell phone." Kurt pulled the phone from his pocket and then set it back in. There was no use getting Laura upset this late at night. He could call in the morning when he knew more about his departure.

"Want a piece?" The cowboy handed him a stick of gum in its foil wrapper.

"Sure. Thanks," said Kurt. He folded the Wrigley in half and set it in his mouth. "You got on the bus in Butte, didn't you?"

"Yup. Finished up on the Ponder Ranch. Where'd you hop on?"

"Dillon. I'm heading to Minneapolis." Kurt slid his hands into his jacket pockets. "My girlfriend is going to have to wait a little longer—it's been three months." For the last two years he'd driven, bused, or flown to Minneapolis depending on how much sleep he'd had, whether his truck was running, or if his boss would give him more than a few days off. Last week's blown head gasket meant a 1000-mile bus trip.

"Ouch," said the cowboy. "That's a stretch. My name is Dodge." He put out his hand.

Kurt shook it, the calloused ridges and thick paw as strong as a wolf trap. "I'm Kurt."

"Pleasure," said Dodge.

The upcoming long bus ride across the rest of Montana, North Dakota and most of Minnesota did not thrill Kurt. Nor did the big city of Minneapolis. Laura was always busy studying, taking classes, or teaching them. Unless Laura was on school break, Kurt always felt as if he was a scheduled appointment. He killed the long hours of the day on walks spanning miles of the city and suburbs, reading in libraries, savoring a cup of coffee at any of the dozens of espresso shops he wandered past. He'd grab a discarded newspaper or magazine and pour over it until his refill was empty.

"Do most cowboys travel by Greyhound now?" Kurt nodded toward the saddle on the floor near Dodge's gear.

Dodge chuckled. "There's a story behind that." He stared at snow blowing horizontally past the window.

"I figured as much," Kurt said. A blanket of snow hit the door and Kurt shrunk back from the blast. His mind drifted to Laura's lithe form hunched over her keyboard, tapping keys for her grad school research. He would reach over to massage her shoulders, nuzzle the nape of her neck. She would tense and then slump her shoulders, encouraging the fingers teasing the knots. "Now's not a good time," she said. He'd keep massaging until she reached to touch his hand. "Okay, but let's make it quick.

I've got a lot of work to do." Kurt knew her as well as the best fishing holes.

"My stomach's growling," Dodge said. "Got some food in my bags. Like jerky?" He strode over to the seats where his saddle, saddle bags, and other gear sat in a heap.

Kurt followed and dragged his pack to where Dodge sat.

"Try this." Dodge handed several blackened strips of dried beef. "Made it myself."

Kurt's jaws worked the tough meat. "This is good. It's got a kick to it."

"That's the secret ingredient," Dodge said. "Red pepper flakes."

"Your secret's out."

"That's about the only secret I have," Dodge said. He shoved the paper sack of jerky back in his bags. "I'm pretty much an open book."

Kurt pulled a gallon Ziploc from his pack. "I've got trail mix. Want some?"

"What's in it?"

"Nuts, M&M's, raisins, granola."

"Sure," Dodge cupped his hands while Kurt tilted the Ziploc's contents into them. "A real potluck."

"You were gonna tell me about a cowboy who rides buses."

"Still want to hear that one, huh?" Dodge stretched out his long frame and parked his legs on the saddle like it was an ottoman.

"Sure."

"I'll make it short and sweet. I like fast horses, fast cars, and—"

"—Fast women?" Kurt cut in.

"I like the slow ones too." Dodge winked at him. "I had me a souped-up '67 Malibu but I guess you could say I had an unfortunate relationship with the highway patrol and their damn radar guns. It doesn't help when you get pulled over after too many Coors. Dee. You. Eye. Three of 'em." He leaned back, staring at the ceiling, the dull yellow of the fluorescent lights cast a shadow on his profile. "This cowboy doesn't have a driver's license anymore. I saddle up my Greyhound now. How about you?" He nudged Kurt's black plastic rod case with his worn boot. "Is this where you keep your magic wand?"

Kurt's rods felt like magic wands. A whipping graphite switch, line whispering through circular guides, fly touching down light as a dust mote, followed by a piscine explosion. Each year since he turned ten, his dad had loaded the Subaru and drove them from Sacramento to fish Montana's fabled rivers. Kurt rowed his first drift boat with an outfitter's clients at eighteen. Twelve years later, the water still cast its spell on him like his first kiss. "There's actually two wands in that case."

"You some kind of pro?"

"I do it for a living, if that's what you mean." The pay wasn't great but the tips were outstanding. His mental data bank of insect hatches, water temperatures, and each hole in southwest Montana rivers, enabled Kurt to coax a fish from a quiet pool under an overhanging bank bristling with willow, or a swift bend like a silver slipstream.

"You're lucky," said Dodge. "It's getting harder to find work. Each spring when the snow finally melts, sleazy realtors pound 'For Sale' signs at the ranches. I worked cattle on the Sparks ranch two years ago and now it's subdivided, cut up like one of those fancy cakes in a Bozeman bakery."

"I guess so," said Kurt. He'd built a reputation, fish by fish, client by client. Dudes with tech or hedge fund cash from the Bay Area, Seattle, New York, or wherever it is people make so much money they don't know what to do with it. More than a few fell in love with the place and were the same folks buying the subdivided land—or the whole ranch. The hills were dotted with monumental log trophy homes sporting forty-foot river rock chimneys. Kurt's dance card filled with "repeat" clients and some brought their daughters along.

* * *

Laura was one of them. Tied to a willow, the boat shimmied in an eddy while Kurt and Laura cast from a gravel bar. Rainbow trout with their black spots and dash of pink iridescence dotted the surface, feeding on stoneflies. Laura plopped a fly right on a big one that shot upstream with it. Kurt was at her side, coaching, praying she landed it. Laura hopped on the bank, flushed with excitement while Kurt waded into the river, netted it, and plucked the fly from the trout's mouth.

"Want a picture with this baby?" Kurt asked.

"Definitely!"

"Kneel in the water and take the fish out for a second." He pointed the camera at her, focusing on the blonde hair spilling over her shoulders. "Got it. Now hold the fish in the water until it swims away." The rainbow's gills fluttered and it eased out of Laura's hands, disappearing with the current.

"That was amazing," Laura said. She gave Kurt a hug, and he dropped his rod on the gravel.

In the evening, after Laura's father had headed to their cabin, Kurt drove Laura in his rattling F-150 to the Blue

Moon, and they spun around the dance floor after two shots of Cuervo.

"Let's have another round. I'm buying," Laura said.

"I'm going to pass," Kurt said. To utter those words tested the limits of his self-restraint. Laura stood in front of him in tight jeans, and maroon and gold University of Minnesota t-shirt. She did not look like a woman who heard that before. "I've got an early morning trip with two guys from Portland. Raincheck?"

Kurt walked back to the bunkhouse after dropping her off and rubbed the spot where she had planted a kiss on his cheek. He didn't know who was doing the catch and release.

* * *

"I'd like to catch one of those realtors in the act of posting a 'For Sale' sign." Dodge made a fist and held it in front of him like a club. "I'd give 'em a good shake. Half of them grew up in the valleys they are selling off faster than tickets at the county fair kissing booth. More like selling their souls." He took his hat off, scratched his head, and put it back on. "I've followed those damn survey lines, touched the wooden stakes with orange flagging, and been half-tempted to rip 'em out of the ground. I'm sick of it—I have to scratch for a ranch hitch these days."

"Sorry to hear that. I really am." Kurt saw Dodge's way of life washing downstream while river bottoms, meadows, and barren slopes filled with homes, trailers, and lodges right up the ridges. He ran his zipper up and down on his pile jacket. "I work so much it's hard to find time of my own. The season used to be May through October," Kurt said. "Now it's just about year-round. We have insulated waders, toe and hand heaters, you name it." Kurt shifted

in his chair. "I have to fight for time off." He and Laura
had many 'discussions' about his lifestyle; she couldn't
understand why he had to work such long hours. "You care
more about your clients or fishing buddies or whatever
they are, than me," Laura said. There was no denying he
wanted to share his love of fishing with them, to see their
wide grins cradling a rainbow before sliding it into the
river. "What about you?" Kurt fired back. "You spend more
time in the lab than some of those rats in their cages." It
hadn't started out that way, but now they were like two
rams butting heads.

"Count your blessings about work." Dodge settled
against the seatback, putting his arms up on it, and looked
at Kurt. "I don't begrudge anyone a living but this is hard
to take. The dudes you take out are spoiling a good thing."

Dodge's words contained a nugget of hard truth. Kurt
wasn't blind to the changes and didn't like everything he
saw either: spiraling real estate prices, commandeered fishing holes, elbow to elbow at the bars. First and foremost,
he was a fisherman—for his own sake. It defined him.
Kurt fished alone long and hard in his off hours, hiking
in blackness to inaccessible reaches by headlamp. It was
a gift to find that spot where it all flowed together: the
near-dawn silence, the lap of water, the first red rays of
light, the accompanying chirp of birds awakening.

"I'm not in it to ruin anyone else's life. I just love what I
do." Kurt popped some trail mix in his mouth. "I wonder
if we're taking better care of the fish but screwing up a
lot of other things in the process."

"Amen to that. As far as fishing goes, I can stick a
worm on a hook and fling it out, hoping something bites,"
Dodge said.

"We don't use worms. We use flies."

"You mean those things that look like the ass-end of a rooster?" Dodge took his feet off the saddle and pulled it toward him, leather creaking.

"Some of the flies have feathers."

Dodge shoved his hat back on his head. "And they catch fish better than worms?"

"They work pretty well, but it's a bit more difficult because we don't have barbs on the hooks."

"Why the hell not?"

"The barbs make it hard to get the fish off the hook." Kurt caught the saddle's earthy smell of leather and horse-hide. He wondered about the hook Laura set. It sure felt like it had barbs.

"Who cares? You clobber it over the head and it is halfway to the frying pan."

"Well, we don't eat 'em."

"What?"

"We let them go. It's called catch and release."

"Now I've heard everything. Closest thing I ever got to that was getting those calves down on the ground and stickin' them with a hot brand. Off they go bawling. No harm comes to them. Except for the castration." Dodge let out a gravelly laugh.

Kurt's hand subconsciously moved to his groin. He wasn't getting his balls nipped but saw his nuts in a vise over what his friend, Derek, called 'this Laura thing.' "Sure, she's hot. Yes, she's super smart. But how's this going to work out," Derek asked, "with you trying to catch every fish in Montana and her staring into a microscope in Minnesota?" Back and forth they went, empty beer bottles lining up on the kitchen table, hashing out romance in general, and Laura in particular. "Face it, you're two cards from different decks." Kurt went to bed convinced it was over. Two days later he was standing in front of the Dillon Greyhound bus stop.

"Ya know," Dodge said, "I get a lot of thinking done on the bus. Kinda get lost in the motor's drone when you're not doing the driving."

"What do you think about?"

"All sorts of things. Growing up. Stuff I'd take back. Things I wished I'd done when I was younger." Dodge's two fingers pinched his upper lip and he held it while his stare drifted toward the wall. He sighed. "When you get to my age, it's harder to change. If I've learned anything, and some would say it hasn't been much"—he tapped Kurt with an elbow—"once you make a decision, go with it."

They sat in silence for a minute and Kurt squinted at his watch: 12:15 a.m. "I'm gonna try to get some sleep." He opened his pack and fluffed up a sleeping bag and laid it across a row of chairs.

"Sleep sounds good," said Dodge. He yanked a worn Pendleton blanket from a saddle bag, set the bag under his head for a pillow, and draped the blanket over him on the adjoining row of seats. "Ya know, there are a lot of things you can change but snowstorms aren't one of them. They're beautiful in their own right so you best ride 'em out and pick up from there."

"That's solid advice," Kurt said.

"Good night, Mr. Fisherman."

"Hope so," said Kurt. Closing his eyes, a vision of a river appeared, pouring across a rock-cobbled bottom. Ahead, the river forked, one side edging a high bank, the other trembled over small boulders scattered willy-nilly in the current. The river disappeared into the mist of sleep.

A rustling sound awakened Kurt.

Dodge was packing his blanket. "Snow's stopped. It's light out and they plowed."

Kurt looked at his watch: 8:15 a.m. "Already?" Rubbing his eyes, he felt a violent need to pee after a restless sleep. He had reawakened at 2:00 a.m. and twisted and squirmed in his bag until after 4:00 a.m. before finally drifting off. "Watch my stuff, okay?"

"Sure."

Kurt headed to the bathroom. The door sign had fallen off and somebody had taken a black marker and written 'MEN' on it. His piss sprinkled off the deodorizing cake. Kurt washed his hands and dried them with paper towels, staring at the nearby condom machine. Colored, flavored, extra-large. He wasn't going to need them.

Dodge sat next to his saddle, his hand on the horn in a gentle caress. "They're boarding in ten minutes. I guess the roads are open. Some kind of miracle, if you ask me."

"I gotta do something." Kurt headed to the ticket window and spoke with the gray-haired lady behind the tiny frame of window.

The driver stowed the luggage in the cargo bay of the bus, but Kurt held back against the wall with his gear. A line of passengers formed by the closed bus door.

Dodge turned around and saw Kurt leaning against the gray cinder blocks. He stepped out of line. "Coming?"

"Nope." said Kurt.

"What about your girlfriend?"

"I guess we're gonna have a long, unpleasant conversation." Kurt didn't relish dialing Laura and breaking the news. There didn't seem like there was any way it was going to work in Minneapolis or any other city Laura did her lab work. It was all a box canyon for Kurt. He couldn't keep this internal tug-of-war going; it was easier to let go of the rope.

"Had a few of those myself," Dodge said. "None of them were fun. One tried to knife me."

The rumbling of the bus started, a cloud of exhaust billowing into the garage. Kurt couldn't alter what was happening in the snow-fed valleys of Montana where multi-hued trout were more valuable than the marbled meat of a grass-fed cow. But he was changing horses in midstream, something no sane cowboy would do.

"I guess this is adios." Dodge shook hands with Kurt. "Next stop, 150 miles east to the hoppin' town of Miles City."

"Thanks for the jerky. Maybe I'll whip up a batch." He hoped Dodge hooked up with a ranch needing a savvy horseman. "Good luck with the highway patrol."

Dodge stepped up on the bus, tipped his hat and disappeared into the darkened interior.

The garage door rattled open and a burst of bright, snow-reflected light forced Kurt to squint. The printing on his ticket looked larger than normal: Dillon. Heading west. Heading home.

FALL, BUCK, AND SCALE

Muffled steps, occasional grunts, and blueberry bushes whapped against their legs, puncturing the silence. Monty followed as Don pushed through brush. Nobody said a word. Heat and sweat built inside Monty's rain gear as it rose from behind his knees, chimney-ed up through his groin toward his armpits and vented out his neck. He self-basted in his rubber outfit as he entered another thicket. Every muscle in his body fixed on the next step he took. Perspiration burned his neck and stung his eyes.

Don packed a chainsaw across one shoulder. It bobbed up and down on his back as he marched across the uneven ground. Matt was a half-dozen steps ahead of Don, shoving branches out of his way with one hand, the other hand clinging to an aerial photo clad in a heavy-duty Ziploc bag. At the back, Monty carried the .375 rifle for brown bear protection. He wished these guys would slow down.

It was like a sea of leaves and a lattice of vegetation they pushed through, climbed over, or crawled under. Periodically, a silver hard hat or a bright yellow Helly Hansen raincoat was visible before it disappeared back into the verdancy bursting forth in a forest with over one hundred inches of rain a year.

Monty entered a small opening next to a trio of towering spruce trees. Matt and Don stared at an aerial photo.

"We're almost there," Matt said.

They were not lost; they knew exactly where they were. It started with the pinprick Matt made in the aerial photo before they left camp. Fifteen minutes earlier, the helicopter had descended into the closest muskeg to the photo's tiny pinhole, and they were now traveling northeast to that spot.

"What's 'almost there' mean?" asked Don. He looked at Matt with an expressionless stare. Don was the faller—he cut down the trees and bucked them into 16-foot logs. He wore an aluminum, wide-brimmed hard hat sitting low on his head, as if his head had been machined to fit it. All you could see were a few wet strands of hair with almost no trace of forehead visible. His gray eyes and aquiline nose gave him a sharp, piercing look.

"Five, ten minutes, maybe."

Monty placed the gun against a tree. "Do you guys always walk this fast?" He used the interlude to catch his breath.

Matt, a sinewy six-foot-three, with a black beard carpeting his face, and Don, a fire hydrant of knotted brawn, were the odd couple of the woods. The one thing they had in common was their ability to maneuver across roots, ravines, downfall, thickets, and stream crossings. How the hell can two guys be so different but travel so quickly? Monty was the guy with the gun and it was all he could do to follow them.

"We actually slowed down," Matt said, "to make it a bit easier on you."

"Wonderful." Monty had been warned when he accepted the Forest Service job in Sitka, and had been handed his Nomex fire-retardant helicopter flight coveralls and a sleeping bag. He had bumped into a bearded dude on his way out the door. As he walked out, the guy asked, "Where you heading, cowboy?"

"Timber sale preparation in Gilbert Bay."

"Oh." The man grimaced. "You must have drawn the short straw. Good luck."

It wasn't immediately clear what the man meant, but he understood now that he was working with Matt and Don. He was their rifle-bearer and go-fer who held the "dumb end of the tape" when Matt measured.

Matt waded into a thorny devil's club patch, their leaves yellow-tinged and drooping. The saw was back on Don's shoulder and he disappeared into the devil's club. Monty picked up the gun and trudged on, hoping they arrived at the pinprick soon.

A few minutes later, Matt held up his hand. "Okay, I think we're almost there."

Monty cradled the rifle in his arm, making a conscious effort to keep the muzzle pointed away from his partners. "Looks like the same stuff we've been walking through for the last five minutes."

"Agreed, but we have to go to the randomly selected plot. Otherwise, we might as well just stop at the most convenient spots and that would mess up all the statistical sampling." In Forest Service parlance, Matt was the "scaler:" the person who measured the trees, looked for rot, and checked the quality of the wood. He was much more than that. Matt managed the small camp, planned the crew's work, and was a master forest navigator.

"Screw the statistics. I'm getting cold. Let's go kill some trees." Don shouldered the saw and started off to the area Matt indicated.

Matt kept walking and looked at the trees. "Okay, this is going to be the center of the plot. Monty, take this can of spray paint and shoot a dot on each tree I tell you to."

Monty turned to look at all the trees around him. "Which tree do you want me to go to?"

"Just start walking and I'll direct you."

"This one over here?" Monty patted the tree and paused at the base of a forty-inch diameter spruce and looked up at it. The first branches were thirty feet above the ground and they kept going up like a giant beanstalk. Moss shrouded the limbs and hung suspended in clumps.

"Yeah, spray that one."

"What about that big sucker behind it?" Don said.

Matt eyeballed the tree. "Nah, that's out."

"Spray it anyway. That's one beautiful tree."

Monty hesitated and looked back at Matt, who shook his head sideways. "Leave it."

For the next ten minutes Monty walked in a clockwise direction spraying trees. Sweat built up again as he made his way through devil's club, skunk cabbage, and blueberry brambles.

After Monty accepted the job offer it occurred to him, he could quietly walk off and never join the crew in Gilbert Bay. Things would be okay—they would find somebody else to do the work. But he didn't want to abandon it. He had disappeared much of his life, an invisible presence in everyone else's story. Too shy at first to make many friends growing up. Too accommodating to those who didn't deserve it. In college, he moved past the uneasy first days of dorm life, trying to figure where he fit in, but the specter of being on the edge of the stage still hovered.

"Okay, that does it," Matt yelled.

"Let's get to work," Don said. He pointed to the first tree he was going to cut and gestured for Matt and Monty to stay back of him in a safety zone. Don pulled the cord and the motor emitted a *WAAAAAAAAA!* blotting out the rest of the world.

Monty and Matt took refuge fifty feet back behind an old hemlock. Don cut a large wedge in the face of the tree, and chips sprayed out in a white stream, piling up rapidly near his feet. He set the idling saw down and gestured to Monty. "I'm gonna let you have the pleasure of knocking your first wedge out of this tree."

Monty walked to Don who pulled a small ax from his pack.

"Take this and give it a whack, Mickey Mantle."

Monty grabbed the ax and took a baseball swing with the blunt ax head. A hunk of pie-shaped wood landed in the chip pile.

"Nice job. We'll make a logger out of you yet. Now head back there with Matt behind that tree until I'm done." Don readied for the back cut and turned around to check on them before starting. The saw bit into the tree, eating through nine inches of wood in less than a minute. He pulled narrow plastic wedges out of his pack and drove them into the cut with the ax head. Watching the top of the tree, Don pulled the saw clear and backed away. The tipping point of a 150-foot column of wood weighing forty tons, changed. It thundered down, smashing two smaller trees in half. Large branches thudded to the ground, the weight and momentum yanking the tree six feet from the stump. The final crash shattered limbs and shook the ground. An eerie silence followed as spruce needles and stray filaments of moss filtered down.

"Right on the money," Don said.

The limbs of the downed tree faced them, spread like giant fans. Don fired the saw up again, walked down the length of the tree, and cut them where they attached to the tree. A geyser of chips and blue exhaust.

While the tree was limbed, Monty counted the stump's rings—all 397, give or take a few. The fallen tree looked like a harpooned whale about to have its blubber removed. Ahab, with his chainsaw, had limbed the tree almost to its top. Monty turned away and looked off through the woods. Moments before, this was a living organism pulling nutrients, water, and light into its bulk. His job was converting it to two by fours.

* * *

Working in Alaska after graduation was a huge leap compared to Monty's normal incremental steps. But the offer was too good to pass up. During his first seasonal stint in the woods earlier in the year, he tasted Alaska: breathtaking scenery, flying in helicopters, camping in the depths of the wilderness. His last crew was a band of adventurers like a cast in an epic-scale play. He wanted more of all of it. And he needed the money after an uninsured drunk totaled his pickup truck. At Gilbert Bay, he wasn't sure of any of it.

Matt looked at Monty. "Our turn. Take this and work your way along the tree." Monty grabbed the end of a fifty-foot logging tape which unspooled from a blue aluminum case attached to Matt's suspenders.

Monty stumbled and climbed over the pile of limbs until Matt yelled, "Stop! Mark it!" Monty chopped a deep gash into the fissured bark. Halfway along the tree, Monty noticed the quiet.

Don had retreated, watching their work from atop the stump, large as the coffee table back in Monty's home in Indiana. He reclined with one arm back propping him up, and the opposite knee up. A cigarette perched in his mouth as he exhaled and tilted his head back like a wolf about to howl. A cloud of smoke floated upward into the mist and dissipated. He had the content look of a man who just got laid.

Matt was busy taking notes and noticed Monty arrive at the treetop, half a football field away. He looked in Don's direction and shouted, "You're up!"

Don flicked the nub of the cigarette butt into a skunk cabbage patch, hopped off the stump, and grabbed his saw. A few pulls and the saw rumbled to life as Monty and Matt pushed foam earplugs in. Don cut chunks of tree out at every mark Monty made. Matt inspected the tree at each cut, scribbling in his yellow notebook about wood defect, quality, and volume.

After several more trees were cut down, Matt looked around and scratched his head with the brim of his hard hat. "I guess it's time for lunch." They huddled under a large spruce providing a roof over them from the mist.

"Damn, I'm hungry." Several large plastic bags emerged from Don's pack, laden with sandwiches, candy bars, apples, crackers, cheese, and cans of pop.

Monty and Don used the spruce as a backrest and Matt sat on a large root. They gobbled their lunches and the talk turned to the remaining work. The chatter faded, and Matt laid down in full raingear with his pack under his head. "I don't know about you guys, but I'm ready for a nap." Taking a cue from their boss, Monty and Don stretched out as well.

Don rolled up his chainsaw chaps and used them as a pillow. "Best part of the job."

Monty awakened to a hard drizzle. He tried to remember why he needed to keep proving himself, and wondered how many seasons it would take before Matt and Don ever thought he was anything other than a go-fer for them.

"Well, I guess lunch break is over," Matt shivered as the last chill from the nap passed.

Don groped for his saw and eyed the spruce sheltering them. "You're next," he said to the tree.

The cutting continued until every large tree in the plot was down and denuded. Monty counted twelve massive trees on the ground, with several other smaller trees shattered, toppled over or otherwise mashed by the behemoths during their brief fight with gravity. The forest floor littered with cut off limbs, emitted the pungent smell of freshly cut spruce and hemlock trees. The carnage lasted six hours and it was too late to do another plot that day. Monty surveyed the destruction surrounding him. It would take a century to fill the hole in the forest they created. Wordlessly, they packed up their sodden gear and walked out the way they came, back toward the landing zone.

Not far from their pickup point, Matt pointed at the ground. "Check that out." A large, steaming pile of bear scat lay in a mound ten feet in front of them. They fell silent knowing the bear couldn't be too far off.

"Did you hear or see anything?" Don asked.

"Nothing," Matt answered.

"Me neither," Monty added.

They all paused and looked around for any sign of the bear that left behind the heap of semi-digested grass and berries, inserting an exclamation point of fear into their march.

"Monty, keep that rifle ready and your eyes peeled," Matt said.

"Did you remember to load it?" Don asked.

Monty gave Don a wry smile. "I'm ready, the safety's off, I have four rounds in the magazine, none in the chamber, and three more in my pocket. Anything else?" Their schedule had them working "tenners:" ten days in the woods in between four days off in Sitka, for the next three months. If this crap kept up, it was going to be a long season.

On the next tenner they slogged alongside a swollen creek to their next plot.

"Shit, that didn't go as planned." The tree Don cut, tottered and wobbled before dumping the butt end into the ground next to the stump. The top was supposed to clear a large spruce 100 feet away. Instead, it hung up in the spruce at a seventy-degree angle with the miscut spruce making a very large hypotenuse.

"Can you cut the bottom and get the top to drop out?" Matt asked. "That could do it."

"Let's take a closer look." Don walked to the tree where the cut spruce was hanging.

Matt and Monty followed Don to the tree. Don stared up at the tree, scanning for some hidden clue unlocking this large wooden puzzle.

"What do you think?" Matt said.

"Monty," Don commanded. "Go get my saw, wedges, and ax."

Uncertain, Monty looked at Matt. It didn't look safe to cut the tree, but Don was confident. Maybe too confident.

"Don't be such a weenie, Monty," said Don. "Get the goddamn saw."

Matt's face pinched with an uncharacteristic tautness to it, "Do you think this is a good idea?"

Don's plan was now apparent. Monty realized Don was going to take down the standing tree with the cut tree looming over the top of him, hoping both trees came down together.

"Just like dominos," Don said.

"The only difference is you die if you lose this game," Matt added in a measured tone.

"Always with the drama, Matt. I've done this before—don't like to make a habit of it though. Monty, go get the saw."

Monty stayed rooted in place, not sure how this was going to play out. The woods were silent; no thrush called, no breeze fluttered the blueberry bushes, no patter of rain.

"We don't need this fucking tree, Don."

"It is part of the plot, right?

"Yeah, but we don't need to take a tree with this level of risk. You're not crazy, are you?" Matt asked.

"Maybe I am crazy or maybe it's a calculated risk."

"Well, Don," Matt said, "I don't like your math."

"The tree is coming down; it's part of the code."

"What code?" Matt asked.

"All trees come to the ground—that's the code." Don gave Matt a pained look suggesting he didn't care if Matt understood or not. Don looked again at Monty. "Are you getting that saw or not?"

Monty went to get the saw.

"You are crazy. You know that, don't you? I could fire you for this, right here, too."

"Fire away, the tree is coming down." Don rummaged in his backpack and pulled a fist-sized spool of parachute cord out. "Here's how this is going to work. I'm going to tie one end of this cord to my suspenders and Matt is going to hold the other end. The two of you will be behind that big hemlock over there." He pointed to a shaggy, moss-covered trunk. "If you see anything funny, pull the cord and I'm gonna run like hell to where you are. That tree is under a shitload of tension from the one hanging up in it so when I start my back cut, I'm gonna really let loose with the saw. It should go right over with that tree leaning on it."

Don yanked the pull cord of the saw and it roared for a second and slowed to a low-throated growl. Matt and Monty scurried to the hemlock trailing the cord, the lifeline to Don. Don drove the saw into the tree with a vengeance. A large wooden chunk plunked out and fell to the ground among a pile of woodchips. The tree hadn't moved, but the dangerous back cut was about to begin. Don looked at the tops of the comingled trees and back to Matt and Monty. Matt gave a 'thumbs up' and Don began the back cut as Matt fingered the cord in his hand. Don immediately pressed the saw's trigger and it ripped through the tree. There was a loud crack, but the tree appeared immovable. The tree made a popping sound and began to teeter. For another microsecond, Don gave the saw everything it had. The mass of branches at the top of the tree levered the tree over and Don tugged the saw from the tree and hurried to the big hemlock for safety. Don squinted at Matt who still had the cord in his hand, their eyes locked momentarily, and they watched the conclusion of his work.

The trees toppled side by side in a cacophonous crash. The ground shuddered and a *Whumpf!* carried across the forest floor like a shock wave. Large limbs crashed to the ground near where Don stood moments before; any of them could have crushed him instantly. Monty and Matt approached the stump, like two bystanders at a car crash.

Don followed, streams of sweat dripping from under the brim of his hard hat. Don handed Matt his end of the cord. "So," Don said, "let's finish the plot."

Back at camp, their hair was still damp after using the propane-fired shower. Dinner call was not far off. The tin stove radiated warm air across the wall tent. The tang of wood smoke mixed with the funk of drying, dirty pants and shirts hanging from nails in the wooden tent frame.

"So, am I fired?" Don was playing solitaire on a small folding table, each card snapping on the table as he played it. His shirt was off, revealing a hairless but powerful physique. Suspenders hung down in a loop from his pants to the floor.

"No," Matt answered. "I know one thing for sure, though."

"What's that?"

"You're one crazy asshole."

"I've heard that before," Don said as he set a king down.

"You seem proud of that."

"Not proud or ashamed if you want it straight up. It's just me. That's the way I am."

Matt set an aerial photo down, rose from his bunk and stood in front of Don. Monty, not sure what was going to happen, put his book aside and watched for any sign of trouble. If it came to that, he knew he would have no choice but to join in. Don was much shorter than Matt, but there was no way Matt's lanky body could handle Don's strength in tight quarters.

Don played another card and looked up at Matt, standing in front of him. "What?"

"Promise you won't pull any more shit like you did today."

Don looked at a card, waited a few seconds. "Agreed."

Matt put out his hand and Don, still seated, shook it. Matt walked back to his bunk, picked up the photo and studied it while Don played another card. Monty, witness to this backwoods détente, picked up his book on the mattress, and tried to find the place he left off.

The rest of their ten-day tour in the woods was uneventful, with each passing day a few less ticks of daylight. More than ever, the four days off seemed to be a pause, an exhalation, everyone on the crew needed. The float plane swooped them away from Gilbert Bay, and forty-five minutes later it taxied on the lapis-colored water of Jamestown Bay in Sitka. Don, Matt, Monty, and two other crew members helped unload their gear from the plane and put it in a big pile of duffle bags, backpacks, and empty fuel jugs on the dock. Don's two large chainsaws dominated the pile; he never left them in the field and babied them like they were twin Stradivari.

It was Thursday afternoon and Matt said to Don, "See you at 8:00 a.m. on Tuesday, right?" It was as if Matt had an unsettling doubt about Don returning to the crew.

Don placed his saws and a duffle in the back of a rusted Ford pickup with one headlight missing and opened the door of the truck. "Yup," was all he said before the truck fishtailed out of the parking lot.

"See what I have to deal with?" Matt said.

"How come you didn't fire him?" Monty asked.

"Good fallers are in short supply. Don's one of the best. He knows it too."

* * *

The late October sunlight had little effect on the chill air pooling around them. Don, Monty, and Matt walked out from the forest with the sound of the approaching helicopter. They crouched in the open and watched it circle overhead.

The helicopter set down in the tiny muskeg at the base of a steep hill that led up to the precipitous flanks of a mountain. Its rubber pontoon floats rocked gently for a few seconds while the rotors flashed over their heads. Eli, their bearded helicopter foreman, jumped out with his helmet visor down, handed everyone Nomex flame-resistant coveralls, and stowed the rifle under the bench seat in the back. Don suited up first so he scooted into the middle with his pack in his lap. Matt and Monty took seats by the door latched shut by Eli. There were three helmets on the back seat and each of them put one on, but only two helmets, those of Matt and Monty, could plug into the two available intercom jacks. Eli climbed in, grabbed his clipboard, and did a quick load calculation. He gave Kirk, the pilot, a thumbs-up they were good-to-go.

The helicopter ascended slowly and cleared a huddle of short, scrubby trees. It climbed a bit more and trembled, like a Maytag on spin cycle, instead of continuing to glide upwards. They sat there suspended momentarily but the shaking only got worse until it became a hard shudder. Kirk feverishly worked the controls. Matt and Monty looked out the window knowing something was not right. A red light flashed on the console followed by a loud alarm buzzing. Small trees loomed below and the helicopter began a very slow descent—each passing second frozen in time.

Kirk yelled into his mic, "We're too heavy. Throw your packs out!"

Monty and Matt opened their doors and tossed their packs out the door. Don, with the biggest pack of all, couldn't hear without an intercom hookup, and was trying to understand what they were doing. Monty ripped the pack out of Don's lap and flung it out the door. For good measure, he reached under the seat and heaved the rifle out the door too.

The helicopter stopped its descent, fluttered momentarily and slowly rose. Monty breathed a sigh of relief. But not enough weight was shed. It lurched forward to another area of the muskeg. If the helicopter settled into the trees, the rotors would rip off, spewing metal shards. When the chopper hit the ground like a wounded duck, it would flop around with an angry turbo-charged engine attached to it. In front of them was a wall of taller spruce the helicopter could not clear unless something radical happened. Everyone's eyes, wide with fear, were on the trees not far below. Kirk's right hand clung to the Cyclic stick and his left hand on the Collective control. He tried to wrestle a mechanical beast at the limit of its capabilities, straining for the last bit of lift left in the rotors.

Monty opened the door and looked down at the spots between the trees and figured it couldn't be more than twenty-five feet down. It was a simple decision. They were going to crash and possibly die unless more weight was unloaded. He unplugged his helmet from the intercom, stepped out on the pontoon and jumped. As soon as he did, the helicopter popped up in the air like a champagne cork, shot out over the trees, and disappeared.

Monty sunk a foot into the cushiony muskeg and his rubber boots were still stuck in the peat while he lay on his side with his stocking feet. He had done a parachutist's landing to help absorb the shock of his fall, something he had learned from a few token skydiving trips in college. He lay panting, staring up into an azure sky, mentally checking if all his body parts were still there. Except for an aching ankle, he was intact. He wrestled his boots out of the mud and put them on, standing up slowly, suspicious of a hidden injury. Limping slightly, he wandered the muskeg retrieving the discarded gear. The rifle was embedded, barrel down, two feet into the mud.

A powerful thirst and chill hit. He grabbed his water bottle and drank when the radio in Matt's pack called his name.

"Monty, Monty, are you okay?" Matt's voice had a tension he had not heard before.

Monty undid the pack straps and pulled the radio out. Before he could respond he got another call.

"Monty, are you there?"

"I'm a bit dazed and have a sore ankle but I'm okay. Where are you guys?"

"We dropped off Don, Eli, and a few items in a muskeg down the hill to lighten our load and did a quick check of the helicopter. Everything seems be working good though. We're gonna come get you ASAP."

Monty looked around the muskeg; the trees stood like silent ghost soldiers in a field and he sat on Don's pack, not caring what squished. His ass was already wet but he didn't want to sit back down on the damp, cold ground. He felt groggy, like the tail end of a hangover settling on him. The adrenaline rush was fading and he wondered if he was going into shock. "How long before you get here?"

"We're in the air now. Should be there in five, max."

"I'm not going anywhere, but I'm starting to get cold. You sure you can find this place again?"

There was a pause and Monty realized how foolish his question was. A muskeg Matt couldn't find? There was no way that could happen—his mind was like one large aerial photo. Matt normally gave a sharp retort to a challenge about his ability to reconnoiter, but given the circumstances he said, "I don't think I'm ever going to forget that spot. Hang on, we'll be there in a bit. I have blankets and a first aid kit too."

Monty draped his yellow Helly Hansen over himself and pulled the hood up. Light slanted through the trees leaving thawed lines across the frost. "Okay, see you in a bit."

The helicopter appeared from behind a low ridge. He saw Matt point to him from inside the Plexiglas bubble as the helicopter cut over the trees at a sharp angle. The helicopter touched down and Monty took a step before he saw Matt hold up his hand to stop moving. This time,

Kirk shut the helicopter down and nobody moved until the blades ceased turning.

Matt approached like he was staring at an alien. "You okay?"

The decision happened quickly but the fall to the ground seemed to suspend him momentarily in the air like an out-of-body experience. In some ways it seemed like a dream now. "All things considered, I guess I am." Monty reached down to pick up a pack.

"Don't make any sudden movement; you may have some internal or spinal injuries." Matt was by his side and put an arm around Monty to escort him to the helicopter.

"I can do this. Let's just take it slow because I think I rolled my ankle."

Kirk walked over to Monty. "I've got 6,000 hours in a chopper but never had a person jump out of one before. You kept that ship," Kirk gestured with his thumb over his shoulder, "from going down. Damndest thing I've ever seen."

It would be hard to explain to anyone. A person casually steps out of a helicopter, like dropping down a rabbit hole, not knowing how badly he was going to get injured. It seemed so unheroic; five people were hitting the ground in a crash if one of them didn't do something. Only he, Eli, and Matt were eligible candidates since Kirk was necessary and Don was in a middle seat. Monty's door was still open from throwing the rifle out so that made the decision clear. Monty surprised himself with the ease of his decision—more a reflex than anything else.

Matt ushered Monty into the helicopter. "Let's head out. We can sort this out back at camp."

Monty lay on his bunk with an ice pack on his ankle, a cup of hot cocoa steaming on an upturned crate next to it. Tylenol dulled the ache creeping into his ankle.

Eli and Kirk, both still wearing their Nomex, pulled the tent flaps aside and came in.

"What the hell happened up there?" Matt jammed another piece of wood into the stove and straddled a folding chair backwards.

"Eli and I have been trying to sort it out," said Kirk. "Near as I can tell we were still within the load limit— just barely. I checked Eli's calculations. And no sign of mechanical issues."

Eli sighed but said nothing. He looked addled as if his body had stopped vibrating and a quiet thrumming had overtaken it.

"There must have been just enough of a downdraft off that peak," Kirk pointed in the direction of the mountain, "and we were so close to the hillside it was like an invisible river flowing that made it hard for the chopper to gain lift." Kirk fiddled with a zipper on his flight suit, opening and shutting a pocket. "Imperceptible. Never seen anything like that."

Monty couldn't help but think back an hour earlier. He had felt that cold air but all it did was chill them while they waited for the helicopter. He had no idea it would be such an insidious force. Would they have died? No way to tell. Maybe burned or maimed; being swathed in bandages and splinted in a critical care ward unnerved him.

Don sat up in his bed, mattress frame springs groaning. "That high dive you took saved us from seriously deep shit."

Monty was so tired he could barely keep his eyes open. In his bewildered state it dawned on him he wasn't sensing friendship. It wasn't camaraderie. As near as Monty could tell, it was kinship. The primitive form of belonging to a tribe. They toiled in the dark forest, slept in the same tent, and broke bread at the same table. Connecting all those dots didn't necessarily lead to friendship. At this point, Monty would take it.

Later that week Matt was looking through the stereoscope staring at aerial photos and he pushed the scope over to Monty. "Check out this plot we're going to tomorrow. What do you think is a good route?"

It took Monty a minute for his eyes to adjust to stereo vision. He saw a possible route up a small ridge from the landing zone. "I think this way could work," as he traced a line with his finger for Matt.

Matt pulled the stereoscope back, "That's what I was thinking, too." His ever-present red grease pencil marked the route.

The following night, Don was sharpening his chainsaw on a homemade bench in their wall tent. The familiar *zzzzzt, zzzzzt, zzzzzt* of the file on the chain stopped. "Why don't you come over here and I'll show you the fine points of sharpening a saw. Might as well learn from a pro."

* * *

At the beginning of November, leaves lay in bunches on the ground, covered in the morning frost. It was too dark to work more than a few hours and camp was shutting down now. In the past three months they crisscrossed this valley dozens of times by air and cursed their way across it on foot.

The helicopter rose from the muskeg for the last time. It moved faster, skimming over the trees and picking up altitude. Monty was between Don and Matt in the back seat, their gear lashed to the pontoon racks.

Monty watched as the valley unfolded below, recognizing the creeks, ponds, and ravines. Obstacles to avoid, not admire. He wished he had stopped more often, soaking in this special place of unending solitude. He paid particular attention to the muskegs since the helicopter left them there to begin the journey to each plot. Many of the muskegs were named based on their shape—the Airport because it was so large; the Catcher's Mitt was circular; and the Needle was so hard to find. Then there was Shithole, where the steaming bear scat stirred their fears.

Monty craned his neck, searching for other landmarks to give context to the immensity of the landscape. Rain ran in streaks across the Plexiglas dome of the helicopter and once or twice, Monty thought he saw a plot, but it was hard to tell since the plot was a speck among the broad expanse of green. The only telltale sign was the tiny clearing and the white of freshly cut stumps visible below.

Don was eating a Hershey bar and holding a half-eaten apple in his other hand. He noticed Monty looking at him, stopped in mid-chew, and gave him a thumbs-up with the Hershey bar. Matt had an aerial photo in his hand, comparing it to the real thing on his side of the helicopter. He saw the thumbs up and glanced at Monty. Matt gave a quick nod and looked back down at his photo.

The helicopter passed the last of the trees and was over slate-colored water. The valley was gone.

THE LAST SCRABBLE GAME
AT BEAVER SWAMP

Reid and Leah recline, backs against a downed log, waiting their turn while the helicopter zips around like a hummingbird, picking up the other Forest Service crews. They'd spent the previous five months laying out a timber sale in this remote Alaskan valley. The radio crackles with a conversation across the valley.

"Rachel, this is Jacob on Channel Three."

"This is Rachel, switch to Channel Eleven."

"Okay. I've got a Scrabble word for you."

"What's the word?" Rachel asks.

"Febrile."

"Feb-what?"

"Febrile. F as in foxtrot, E as in echo, B as bravo, R as in Romeo, I as in India, L as in Lima, and E as in echo," spells Jacob. "It's a killer word with three vowels and nothing special for consonants. If you play all seven tiles, though, it's a fifty-point bonus."

"Where the hell did you find a word like that?"

"I read the dictionary looking for seven-letter words not too far out in difficulty."

"I'll keep it in mind," Rachel adds.

"Hey guys," Reid chimes in. "Let's save the radio batteries for meaningful conversation such as pickup locations or emergencies. I've got some words for both of you, but I'll save them for later." They won't take him to heart. He chuckles at some of the crazy shit his crew does. This isn't the first time Scrabble words were discussed over the radio with the latest topic covering words with 'Z' and 'X'. Until last week, he had no idea a zax was a tool for trimming slate shingles. He looks at Leah, shakes his head and mutters, "Jesus" before shoving the radio back into his sodden pack.

Jacob is back on the radio. "Don't worry, Reid, I've got some good words for you too."

Leah flashes him two raised eyebrows with the unstated message: You started this. Not much we can do about it now.

* * *

Even with Scrabble occupying his crew, life is so much simpler at Beaver Swamp than it had been for Reid back home. He graduated college with a forestry degree, Boilermaker Class of 1978. Not long afterwards, his parents divorced and sold the Indiana split-level home he'd grown up in, moving to different parts of the country. No warning, no idea it was coming, as if the warranty on their marriage expired. He had no siblings to share his dismay or to learn if there were signs he missed. A bloodless wound, festering. The anger turned into questions. The questions turned to emptiness, and the emptiness turned to flight.

There were long rides with people who had no business being on the road in the vehicles they were driving. "I'm living from gas station to gas station," confided Carl, the driver of an ancient, battered green Ford pickup. "If this thing dies, I'm setting off on foot." Two hours later they both had their thumbs out, the family Scrabble box wrapped in plastic and strapped to Reid's pack.

Or the drivers had no business being on the road in their condition. The dented Dodge pulled over, leaving a plume of dust behind it. Rope held the hood down. A man in faded denim and an untucked flannel shirt rolled the window down. "Hop in, I can take you as far as Watson Lake." He handed Reid a beer through the window although it was only 9:00 a.m.

Reid saw five empties on the floor and the rest of the case was in the backseat. "How about I give you a break and I'll drive?"

The man opened the driver's door, tumbled out onto the gravel, and staggered to the rear door. He opened the door and stretched out on the back seat, right on top of the beer, and fell asleep before Reid hit forty miles per hour.

* * *

A raven caws as it passes in the shadow of peaks rising steeply from the valley floor, and over dense stands of hemlock and spruce. The call fades and Leah and Reid step from a cluster of trees into an open area, listening for a different kind of bird. From the other end of the valley, the *whop, whop, whop* of helicopter rotors is faint but growing stronger by the minute.

"I hear it," says Leah. She puts her hand above her eyes to block the sun as it slants through the parting clouds. As she steps across a rivulet in the opening, one shoulder strap on her bib rain pants slides off her shoulder. The checked wool Pendleton shirt she wears has two elbow patches on it, recent additions sewn on by lantern light. Reid places bright orange flagging on the ends of a scraggily tree limb to help the pilot find them and show the wind direction.

The chopper searches as it turns to make another pass. "Uphill and to your left," Leah directs via radio, and Reid stands up. He is stripped down to a logger's shirt, waving his yellow raincoat like a deserted island survivor trying to attract a passing freighter. The helicopter angles at them and they crouch low, away from the landing zone. Dead grass, spruce needles, and twigs zip by them from the rotor blast, and they cover their eyes with their hands for protection. The Plexiglas-domed chopper resembles a large dragonfly. In a minute it lands, and they hunch over into the wind with the turbine screaming.

A Forest Service helicopter foreman jumps from his seat next to the pilot as they reach the ship, and hands them two green, Nomex fire-resistant coveralls and helmets to wear. Blades cleave the air a few feet over their heads. They cram arms and legs into the flight suits, the foreman stows their bear protection rifle under the back seat. "Is that everything?!" the foreman screams. Reid gives him the thumbs-up.

In the backseat, chest harnesses snap, helmet cables click into intercom jacks, backpacks lay heavy on their laps. From his front seat, the foreman looks them over and says into his mic to the pilot, "We're good." With an explosion of energy, the chopper rises and slaloms downhill over the trees, like some high decibel sleigh.

Over the intercom, Bill, the pilot, says, "Next stop, Beaver Swamp."

On Leah's side are tall summits with a white snowline; winter is not far off. Reid's view from the "downhill" side of the helicopter reveals a five-mile-long valley, filled with ponds and beaver marshes sitting in a bowl, before the mountains surge upwards on the other side. The sun turns the beaver ponds into mirrors. Two tundra swans send concentric circles rippling outward in one pond. Reid taps Leah on the thigh, their eyes catch for a moment. Her dark brown hair is hidden by the helmet she is wearing, which accentuates her round cheeks and dark brown eyes surrounded by a cue-ball whiteness, making her irises stand out.

Their season is over and it's one of the last helicopter flights they'll take together before camp closes in the next few days. The pangs of not sharing more time with Leah catch Reid in the gut. Together, they've beaten through brush, gasped up hills, laughed at embarrassing gaffes— when Leah fell face-first in the mud or Reid inhaled a cloud of no-see-ums. They fended off mosquitoes, swatting them off each other's back, and huddled against chilling rain. She is more than a work partner and he doesn't want to lose her. He hopes she feels the same way. The hard part is finding the courage to speak. It's an all or nothing choice; if he spills his feelings and she's not interested—it's over. Everything they have now will be spoiled.

* * *

Back in August, Leah and Reid had slumped side by side next to a lunch fire warming their feet under the awning of a large spruce. Damp wool socks hung drying from branches next to the coals.

"I love this place," Leah said. A rain drop from her Helly Hansen jacket hood plopped on her nose.

"What do you mean?" Reid cracked a branch over his knee and placed it in the fire.

"It's so quiet and peaceful. You can almost hear yourself think. I've never felt this way anywhere else."

Reid was blessed to work with Leah. She was unflappable in the face of cold, wet, mud, hunger, and fatigue. Gracefully skipping across creeks, balancing on a rock while water hissed by. Or scampering along a downed tree like a marten.

Reid worked with others on his crew periodically, but the best days were the ones with Leah. He was in charge of a collection of poorly dressed, foul-smelling seasonal employees traipsing around the woods marking potential roads and trees to be cut. There was this unspoken barrier with Leah, like a fine mesh they could see through but kept them from physically getting closer to each other. More than that though, he respected her; she had an equanimity that carried over to everyone she was around as if she had telepathically slipped them a Valium. They tiptoed up to that invisible line many times but never crossed it.

Leah pulled out a gallon Ziploc bag and grabbed a peanut butter and jelly sandwich.

"What's for lunch?" Reid asked.

"PBJ, it's a bit mashed, though."

"I've got turkey—it's also taken a beating in my pack. Why don't we mix and match?"

"Deal." Leah handed him half a sandwich with jelly oozing out of it.

They munched quietly, toes resting on a small log near the edge of the fire. The heat worked its way into their limbs.

"I've seen your toes so many times I've got names for them," Leah said, "so you're going to have to name mine."

"You do? Like what?" Reid asked.

"You tell me first."

Reid was puzzled but took a stab at it. "That left big toe is Zelda."

"Zelda?! Where did you come up with that?"

"It just came to me."

They burst out laughing and never named the rest of her toes.

* * *

Reid points to the swans and she nods. From their vantage point in the helicopter, there is no road, no town, not one house or light visible. Just south is a long fiord with cliffs rising thousands of feet straight out of the water. Icebergs from the glacier at the head of the fiord floated for thirty miles and lay grounded in the shallow bay.

The helicopter veers left. An opening in a furrow of trees appears, and the only habitation in the entire lowland comes into sight—Beaver Swamp. There is nothing impressive about the five wall tents on plywood platforms; three are for sleeping, one is for gear storage, and the cook tent, across the clearing. Maximum population during the peak of summer: twelve people.

The helicopter glides over the trees and settles on the ground. Bill cuts the power and the rotors come to a stop. "Well, that's it for today." He is a trim Vietnam War vet with an odd sense of formality and tidiness. He takes great pride in being clean-shaven and having a sharp crease in his flight suit every day in a place where personal appearance is never a priority. Every evening, he closes out the day like a news anchorman with the same comment.

They trudge sixty yards to camp through boot-sucking mud and wet grass. As they approach the tents, Jacob steps out. He and his partner, Randy, were picked up before Reid and Leah. Jacob has already showered. His dark hair is matted from the water and his slight build, thin, angular face and scruffy beard make him, along with his metal-framed glasses, look like a grad student at an ivy-covered college.

Reid sits against the edge of the tent platform, relieved to be done. It is that point in the day between fatigue and the sense of accomplishment from stumbling around the woods, finding obscure points on an aerial photo like they're on a topographic treasure hunt. The mental toll of getting everyone back each day in one piece frays him. Slips down steep hillsides, branches whipping eyeballs, chainsaws slashing through chaps. He pulls off his boot and a wet sock comes with it, when Jacob sidles up to him and hands him a cup of hot cocoa with little marshmallows bobbing in it.

"How'd it go today?"

"Not bad. A shower will definitely help." Reid tosses the boot, and it skitters across the floor.

"So, what are you doing once camp shuts down?" Jacob asks.

"I have office work to do for a month before I get laid off for the season. I'm thinking about holing up in a nice ski town in the Rockies for the winter. Maybe Telluride. I've got a few buddies down there that will let me sleep on their couch." Reid knows there will be a lot of competition for that couch too, since at least a few other friends have turned their mental compasses to Telluride for the off-season. "Mexico sounds good too. I'm hearing about some places on the Pacific side." The beach, heat from the sand seeping into him, and a cold beer by his side, is a notion rapidly gaining appeal. Even better would be Leah on a towel next to him.

"Hey, maybe I'll come with you. I know some Spanish."

"You told me you were going to visit your parents and then go back to school for the spring semester." Jacob had shared many tales of his family vacations, holidays together—chestnuts roasting over an open fire type of stuff—and how close he is to his sister, Janey. "I'm sure your mom, dad, and Janey would love to see you and I'll bet they want you to finish college."

"You're probably right," Jacob says. "So many expectations. Where's the spontaneity, the serendipity in life? You're going to be slicing through deep powder while I'm stuck in a formaldehyde-filled lab with preserved animals in it. All those beady eyes staring, crying out for Latin name identification." Jacob rolls his eyes and grimaces. Changing the subject, Jacob brightens. "Ready for the game tonight?"

"As ready as I'll ever be," Reid says. "I'm in third place behind Rachel and Randy." Reid thought back to the day he walked into the cook tent with his family's Scrabble game. An evening diversion for his crew.

It had been a distraction for his parents during their failing marriage. One of Reid's few memories of his parents doing anything fun together was their weekly Scrabble game. His father hunched over his rack of tiles, scotch in hand. His mom pulled the rack onto her lap and laid back on the sofa, wine glass on the coffee table. As much as they were a mismatch in life, they matched up well on the score sheet.

One evening in July he had brought it into the kitchen tent after dinner. "Anyone wanna play Scrabble?" There were only three people in the tent at the time: Rachel, Randy, and Jacob.

Jacob was whittling a stick. "Not tonight, Reid."

Randy set down the cards from his fifth game of solitaire. "I'll give it a shot. It's been a long time though." Randy was normally Jacob's field partner and the camp curmudgeon. Jacob and Randy argued over who took a wrong turn up a creek, forgot to bring enough flagging, or didn't pack a big enough lunch, but then the squall blew over, much like the weather they faced together each day.

"Count me in." Rachel swept a pile of magazines, books, candles, empty pop cans, aerial photos, and a bowl of chainsaw parts with her forearm from her side of the plywood table. Randy dragged his chair toward Rachel's end.

"So how do you do this again?" Randy asked.

"We each select seven tiles," Reid said.

Little did anyone know this was the beginning of one the longest running board games in the history of Alaskan field camps.

* * *

Reid tilts his head in the direction of the shower, just beyond the cook tent. "Anyone in the shower?"

Jacob mumblety-pegs his knife into a log. It bounces off, and he bends to pick it up. "I think it's open, but you'll have to hurry."

There is no roof to the stall and the water comes from a black plastic pipe running two hundred yards uphill to a creek. The pipe is plumbed into a propane hot water heater next to the stall for showers—hot and cold running water in the middle of nowhere.

Reid strips, stands on the wooden pallet outside the shower, kicks off his flip flops and turns the water on. The hot water cascades off his scalp and he hangs his head while rivulets run down his body. His thoughts turn to Leah as the water funnels down his groin and a hollowness grows inside him. He shuts his eyes and leans his head on the shower stall, the only thing propping him up now, as the heat and steam separate him from his surroundings.

"Hey! Whoever's in the shower, make sure to save some hot water for me." Leah's calling out from a few feet away snaps Reid out of his trance faster than if the cold water had suddenly started flowing.

"Be right out," Reid says, not realizing he was hogging the hot water.

"Is that you in there, Reid?"

"Yup."

"All I can say is…," Leah pauses for effect and Reid can practically see her in the tattered flamingo-pink cotton bathrobe she wears to the shower. Her lone trace of femininity. "You're lucky it's me who found you camping out in there and not the Lezs. They would have dragged your sorry ass right out."

* * *

It had been late April when Reid had been sitting in his office behind a scarred metal desk staring at a faded piece of paper with typewritten names on a list. It was a list of people he hired from the official government personnel register. He had no way to tell how any crew would work out; would they gel or make life hellish for him? He absentmindedly picked up a pair of scissors and cut each name out of the list: Jill, Jacob, Randy, Rachel, and Leah. The little pieces of paper slid around under his finger, and he matched up prospective pairs of names for work partners, switched them, and moved them again trying to imagine a winning combination.

Jill and Rachel are the camp lesbians who share one of the wall tents and unabashedly call themselves "The Lezs." Reid was blessed to have Jill and Rachel on the crew, and nobody really gave any thought about their sexual persuasion. They always showed up for work on time, knew where they were going in the field the next day, and took care of their gear. Guys—they beat the shit out of their equipment. Chainsaws came back with pull cords hanging out like dog tongues, chains busted, or the bars inexplicably bent. The Lezs chanted, "Estrogen rules!" whenever a guy broke something by trying to overpower it.

* * *

Rachel sets up her rack and mixes the upside-down tiles inside the box cover while Randy clears the rest of the table. Reid knows Leah is in her tent and usually makes an appearance during the Scrabble game. He waits in anticipation, like a hunter trying not to breathe too hard. He feigns calmness but inside tautness grips him. It's a new feeling, a blend of helplessness and intoxication.

"Pick a tile," Rachel says. Whoever picks the letter closest to 'A' gets to pick their seven tiles first and go first.

Randy selects a 'C.' "Top that." Reid knows Randy is thrilled because he needs every point he can get and whoever goes first gets double points.

Rachel reshuffles the tiles with their blank faces staring at her and draws a 'P.'

Reid grabs an 'S.' Aside from trailing in points and thinking about Leah, his focus is on camp closing tomorrow after a long season that started in mid-May. Reid was part of the three-person crew dropped off to build the camp named Beaver Swamp. Now, in late October, daylight is much shorter, and the crews are lucky to get six hours of work in the woods, particularly in the dusky gloom of the coastal rainforest. The alder trees are bare while the ferns that spread so mightily in early summer now lie in brown bundles. On clear mornings, the frost settles thickly on the grass, and the creeks and beaver ponds are rimmed with ice.

Several days will be needed to break camp and haul all of the materials by helicopter down to the bay, where a landing craft and De Havilland Beaver float plane will rendezvous with them. The skeletons of the tent platforms are all that will be left—they will make it through winter and be needed next year so the timber sale can continue to be laid out.

Once camp break-up starts there will be no time for Scrabble so tonight is the final game. The board has been unfolded seventeen times and nobody has won a game yet; they decided at the end of the first game that they would keep a running score and Rachel leads with 2,721 points to Randy's 2,670 points, and Reid's 2,540.

* * *

"I'll grab my tiles now," Randy says with a satisfied smile. He stares at the backs of seven tiles as if each one held the key to the winning word. He randomly plucks his tiles and sets them in his rack. Inwardly, he grumbles; five out of seven letters are low-point vowels.

Rachel is less deliberate and picks her tiles. Almost all of them are consonants. She mixes them around in her rack to see what potential word combinations are available.

Randy places three tiles at the center of the board: 'gun.' "Four points times two on a double word score." He will have to do better, or it will be a long night.

Jacob says, "With big words like that you're ready to write the next great American novel."

"You saw what I had to use." Randy picks three new tiles and sighs, "That's much better."

Randy is not known for the biggest words, but possesses an innate ability to use low-scoring tiles in tight spaces to generate points where not much opportunity exists. The more congested the board gets, the better he is. Rachel goes for high-scoring, big words so it is the home run slugger against the singles hitter with the high batting average. Reid's strategy is somewhere in between.

Rachel shifts some tiles around on her rack and places five on the board attached to 'gun.' "Flagon. F-L-A-G-O-N. That's nine points."

"What the hell's that?" Randy asks.

"It's an old word for a container that holds liquor or some kind of alcohol," Rachel says.

Jacob shakes his head. "Impressive."

A few minutes pass and Randy arranges tiles, trying to make sense of them.

Rachel is reading a magazine waiting for Randy. "Ready?"

"Yup." Randy plops four tiles and attaches them to the 'N' on 'flagon.'

"'Hymen.' That's thirteen points." Randy smiles, knowing it's a good word and that it's slightly naughty—nothing like getting points and tweaking Rachel at the same time.

Jacob says, "I thought this is a family game."

"Jacob," Reid joins the fray, "this camp is full of perverts and if you just learned that, then I don't know where you've been all season. It's the only thing that keeps us sane out here."

"Okay, I'm ready with my next word: 'balls.'" Rachel acts as if she is going to place the tiles and then says, "Don't worry, I'm just kidding. I wouldn't waste a precious 'S' on 'balls.'"

Leah enters the tent, and it is like pumped-in oxygen. Reid inhales and breathes in again, and he can feel his face flush. She scans the board and her eyes stop at 'hymen.' "Looks like we're getting an anatomy lesson tonight."

"Is it hot in here or is it just me?" Reid says.

"Look," Randy defends, "it's a legal word and it's all I had in my rack. Let's just get on with the game."

Leah hunches over and puts her face close to Rachel's in that girl-friendly way that knows no interpersonal space. "Are these boys picking on you?"

"They are and they're making me cry," whines Rachel in her best little girl voice.

Leah scowls at Jacob, Randy, and Reid. "Who's in charge here? It must be you."

She squints at Reid.

Reid slowly uncrosses his legs and stands up. Randy and Rachel quickly cover their racks so Reid can't see their tiles. He approaches Leah and in his best John Wayne imitation says, "Ma'am, I am the law in these parts. If you or this other fair maiden need protection, you can count on my services." He doffs an imaginary cowboy hat. "In the meantime, why don't you head over to the kitchen and make some brownies for us hard-workin' Scrabble players." He steers her by her shoulders to the propane range at the other side of the tent.

"Oh sheriff, I'm gonna swoon." Leah holds her forearm to her head. "I'll do anything you say."

Reid winks at Leah. "Anything?"

Leah bats her eyelids. "Sheriff, just what kind of services are you offering?"

"Leah, go bake the damn brownies already," Randy breaks in. "We've got a game to play here."

Leah salutes and starts rummaging in the kitchen for the ingredients.

The game goes on for an hour and grows quieter as the tiles click, and the players survey the board looking to crowd a few tiles in and squeeze a few points out. Jill ambles in, feels the force of the concentration, grabs a brownie, and silently gives Rachel a high five before departing. Jacob and Leah drift off to their tents. Reid has turned his rack over and conceded, and is absentmindedly eating a brownie. He goes outside for a minute when he hears Rachel exclaim, "Kiss my ass!" Randy lets out a low groan like an accordion deflating and he knows the game is over. He hears Rachel shuffling in the tent and through the tent wall he sees the silhouette of her dancing a spastic jig.

"Girl, you just wait 'til next year. I'll be ready for the rematch."

"Well," Rachel crows. "Then I hope you'll be ready for Kiss My Ass, Part II!"

Reid pauses and smiles, drinking in his crew's camaraderie. He continues gingerly across the muddy grass to his tent when he hears a voice quietly say, "Hey." He hadn't noticed Leah standing in the dark in front of her tent that she shares with an assortment of hand tools, scrap wood, and spare sleeping bags. He walks over, the ground squishing with every step.

"Looks like we have a winner," Leah says.

"I thought you went to bed."

"Nope. Just thinking." Leah's arms are crossed over her chest to ward off the chill.

"About?"

Leah doesn't answer right away. "I was thinking about staying on and helping close up camp."

"I thought you were going to take off with Jacob and the Lezs while Randy and I put this place to bed for the winter." Reid stands directly in front of Leah with his arms crossed and their chilled breath merge, leaving a fog hanging over them.

"Changed my mind. I can do that, right?"

"I don't see why not. I'll check with Randy in the morning, but I don't think he'll care since he's anxious to get back to town anyway."

Leah reaches and touches him on his bicep, and he can feel the warmth of her hand through his shirt. She leaves it there for a few seconds, looks at him with those carbon-dark eyes, leans forward and kisses Reid on the lips, before slipping her arms around him. The strawberry scent of her shampoo wafts over them, and a small earring brushes his cheek while the press of her breasts reveals a heart beating harder than his own. They cling to each other wordlessly, oblivious to the cold, the camp, the stars.

Leah pulls away slowly although Reid could have stayed in that position until the sun thawed him. "Thanks, Reid." She opens her tent flap and starts to go inside when she pauses, "By the way, I already talked to Randy and he's fine with our new arrangement." She doesn't wait for an answer and goes inside.

Reid jolts awake—the glowing dials on his clock show 3:11 a.m. He's not aware what stirred him, and lies in bed, startled by his lucidness. He slowly unzips his sleeping bag and quietly pulls on a sweatshirt and sweatpants so he doesn't wake Jacob out of his low-RPM snore. Randy lays noiseless, his chest gently rising and falling, while Bill's only sign of life are tomorrow's clothes set out neatly on his footlocker.

He parts the front door flaps. Must be twenty-five degrees. A few scattered clouds pass by the moon and Reid sees the glint from the dome of the helicopter and the grass, silvered by the heavy frost, in the illuminated camp. The silence is as clear and palpable as his breath suspended in the air.

The clouds converge and a shadow lingers over camp. Reid imagines Scrabble tiles and words drift through his mind. They shift and change, then all new tiles appear. The game goes on, and always will. They're all players choosing their own tiles and laying them down as best they can.

WALKING OUT

Matt presses the mic button on the radio, "Gilbert Bay, we're ready for pickup." The only response is the scolding *chit-chit-chit* of a squirrel from a nearby branch.

"Try again," Don says.

"Gilbert Bay, this is Dickens on Channel 3. We're ready for pickup."

Too tired to stand, I squat on my haunches, not wanting to sit on the cold ground. Mud streaks one side of Matt's face and a red welt rises on the other side where a branch smacked him. A spray of woodchips laces Don's shirt.

"So where are they?" Don asks.

"Call one more time," I suggest.

With a burst of static, the radio comes to life. "Somebody calling Gilbert Bay?" It's Walt, the helicopter pilot.

"Gilbert Bay, this is Dickens on Channel 3," Matt pauses for a moment. "We're ready for pickup."

"There's a problem at our end," Walt says. "I'm getting some kind of warning light in the cockpit, and I can't fly until I get this sorted out. I've been working on it the last hour so I didn't hear your call."

"So, what does that mean?"

"You need to hike back to camp," Walt says.

"Shit!" Don rips the hard hat off his head and Frisbees it into the woods. It sails through the trees, careening into a spruce before disappearing in a blueberry thicket.

"What's the plan?" I ask.

"The plan is," Matt looks me in the eye, "we walk."

Matt looks off in the direction of Don's hard hat. "You're gonna need that."

"I know, but it's a solid six miles to camp and I'm packing this goddamn saw. Monty, you saw where the hard hat landed, didn't you? You get it," Don demands.

"You threw it, you get it," I respond.

"Don, get the damn hat," Matt cuts in. "Let's get this show on the road."

Don grumbles and tromps off into the tangle of green.

"Found it!" Don holds the hard hat triumphantly aloft.

* * *

The three of us are a Forest Service timber sampling crew working in the depths of southeast Alaska's Tongass National Forest. We are so far off the grid we might as well be on another planet. Don is our faller. Aside from being our boss, Matt measures the cut trees in the plots we sample, and I'm the "go-fer" who packs the .375 rifle for brown bear protection.

I struggle matching these woods warriors passing through the forest with the ease of animals. Don is short with a body of coiled muscle and Matt is tall and rangy. It's a long walk back to camp and I wonder if I can keep pace. Trees tower over me, blocking the sky in a dizzying kaleidoscope of green canopy.

I've worked with these guys for six weeks and it isn't always a ton of laughs. I'm new to Alaska and while I'm here for the adventure, the money's not bad either. The hard part is fitting in with my coworkers who show little tolerance for rookies or in my case—a "flatlander"— since I'm from Indiana.

I zip my jacket in the chill of early afternoon. "Which way?"

Matt hunches over, staring at the aerial photo. To me, the photo is a blank page filled with blurs, and light and dark areas. Some parts are easy to spot: lakes, the coastline, and mountaintops, but to divine a route avoiding acres of downed trees, steep ravines, or beaver swamps takes skill and practice. When it comes to maps and photos, Matt "sees" the subtleties in a slope or the slight change in tree size. Transforming these flat objects into three dimensions in his mind, it's like he mentally walks the route before ever setting foot on it.

Matt's focus is on getting our sample plots done before field season is over. He presides over a small camp of people laying out a timber sale: surveyors placing wooden stakes for potential roads, crews marking harvest units, and us. I see his steadiness and calm, laying out everyone's work, and managing camp logistics, and I can't tell if he enjoys the job. His dark eyes reveal little and there is no tolerance for slackers and whiners. I want to see my boss let loose, but his smiles are rarer than a sunny day in southeast Alaska.

Matt points to the photo, "I think we should get to the beach where the walking will be better. We're gonna work our way through the woods for a while instead of going straight because the short way is hellish, and my way is just plain shitty."

"I think we should go straight and get this over with," Don suggests. "Or just hole up in the woods for the night until the chopper gets us." Don is like an AK-47, safety off and one in the chamber. He's contracted to fall trees—period—and does as little in camp to help as he can. It's like being around a downed high-tension line.

"Too steep—the chance of someone getting hurt is higher the short way," Matt says, "so that's out."

"What about holing up?"

"You ever been stuck in the woods before?" Matt asks.

Don readjusts one of his suspenders. "Once."

"How'd it go?"

"It sucked."

Spending the night in the woods doesn't foster fond memories for me either. Years ago, our Boy Scout leader got lost and we hunkered under our ponchos for the night while a thunderstorm flashed, and a cutting rain strafed us for hours. To cover his ass, the next day he told us it was "emergency bivouac" training. Under the best of circumstances, a night out without proper gear in Alaska in mid-October will be cold, sleepless, and definitely miserable—even if we manage to keep a small warming fire going.

"What do you think we should do, Monty?" Don asks.

"I'm with Matt; I'd rather keep moving than camp out."

"Besides," Matt adds, "there's no guarantee the helicopter will be fixed tomorrow."

"Oh alright, I might as well go with you guys. I don't want to freeze my ass out here alone."

We walk and tendrils of heat work their way back into my body after the long break. The first stretch follows a deer trail meandering along the base of a long hillside before ascending and dropping to the other side. In places, trees crashed across the trail, forcing us to route around them, often into layers of brush before we are back on the trail. As we wind back up a long hill, I'm in a stand of immense trees with a clear view through the woods—a rarity in a verdant rainforest—and stop to take a 360-degree picture for my memory. It reminds me of why I came to Alaska: awe-inspiring trees, luminous snow-covered mountains, and vast stretches of wilderness.

"Hey, break time is over!" Don's voice cuts across the gap between us while I am tree-gazing. I hurry to catch them and Don offers to Matt, "Mark this place on your photo for a future plot—there's a lot of volume to cut here." That's Don's thoughtful way of erasing my memory with his chainsaw.

The trail evaporates and we are in a clawing lattice of blueberry with several large fallen trees. The pace slows and my breathing gets heavier as I grab and push brush, looking for the path of least resistance. An occasional "shit" or "fuck" comes from Don who has the worst of it carrying the chainsaw. Matt and I grunt periodically before I get yanked to a stop when my rifle sling snags on a branch. Matt's hands are white and shriveled from the damp cold. There is no talking—it is just a slow onward surge through the vegetation. I bump into one bush, and it dumps a load of cold water down my neck; it seeps past my shoulder blades, leaving a damp spot by my belt line. "Damn."

Finally, we find a well-worn deer trail and break into an opening in the forest with small bonsai-like trees and waterlogged ground—better known as a muskeg. The route follows a game trail, and the deeply embedded tracks of bears leave unmistakable flattened depressions in the moss where paws have been placed for generations. About halfway across the muskeg Matt stops to review the photo. "Don, drop your saw here. We'll come back for it when the helicopter can fly."

"I've never left my saw in the woods—ever."

"Do you want to pack it another five miles?"

"Not unless I have to."

"This is the only muskeg big enough for a chopper to land between here and the beach," Matt says. "It's now or never."

"What about the three of us switching off with the saw? That way nobody will get tired. Monty can take it first."

"We need to move fast, and that saw is an anchor no matter who is carrying it." Matt takes off his hard hat and scratches his head.

Don looks around the woods for a few seconds and plops the saw on the ground. I'm thrilled not to sling the heavy Stihl chainsaw over my shoulder.

"Well, I guess it's settled." Matt pulls a roll of fluorescent orange flagging from a vest pocket. He hands me flagging and points to a scraggly pine in the middle of the muskeg about thirty yards ahead. "Flag the hell out of that tree over there. Make sure it's something we can see from the air."

Shortly afterwards, we find ourselves on a bluff's edge and slant down it, moving along a distinct game trail. The angle steepens and we hear water rushing far below us. It is not much further before we stare from a rocky outcrop overlooking a deep ravine. Not really a cliff, but a lot more than a steep hill. Matt bites his lip. "Wish I had a rope in my pack."

The drop is so sharp we can almost walk out on the treetops below us.

Matt says to Don, "How'd you like to be packing a chainsaw there?"

"No fuckin' way."

"Any other route?" I ask.

"Believe it or not, this is the least of all evils." Matt cinches his shoulder straps.

"Just take this slow," Matt tells us. "Don't crowd, and pass the rifle to the guy below when you need to."

Don goes first. He tests each foothold before putting his full weight on it. There are roots and he grabs a small tree on the way. "Good so far."

I follow Don's route and lower the rifle to him at one spot where I need two hands to hang on to the slope. I wish I had three hands and four legs and make a point not to look down. Soon, we are standing on a small platform at the base of a tree—the only place flat enough before continuing. Don leaves the ledge to create a place for Matt, and maneuvers along a wall of moss-covered rock.

There is no space large enough for us to take a break so Don continues down. I watch from above and mimic his movement. I see a small seep oozing from the ground. Don takes one step and I hear a *Whooooaaa!* from below. Luckily, Don catches himself with some nearby branches and comes to a stop eight feet below the slip. Don cups his hands to his mouth and yells over the din of the creek, "Slippery—watch that spot!"

I consider my options. Farther down, the creek is a blur of white like a never-ending freight train. For a second, a wave of dizziness flashes and my stomach roils like it is ready to flip.

I head left and am surprised to find a small series of hand and footholds, not visible from above. In a minute, I'm standing next to Don, the shaking in my thighs subsiding.

Matt joins us and we all look at the stream in front of us, running bank to bank with rainfall over the last few days. Upstream is a pinched ravine with a torrent pulsing like a fire hose. Fifty yards downstream the creek disappears over a ledge.

Matt points up the ravine. "Look." A large fallen tree spans the entire creek.

Don sprints to the tree. "Just what we ordered." He climbs the tree and starts walking across, using its dead limbs like a handrail. Halfway across, a doormat-sized piece of bark slides out beneath his foot, and he is in the creek bobbing and rolling, pushed by the current. Instinctively, I drop the rifle to the ground and charge into the water—over my boot tops—and latch on to Don's arm just as he's almost past me. I feel the current ripping Don away. Don's fingers clamp around my forearm while my fist is full of his jacket. With one last heave, I lurch backwards, and we stumble into the shallows of the creek. We're dripping and adrenaline-fueled, but know it will wear off and the cold will send in its cloak of hypothermia.

I'm soaked to mid-thigh and ice water flows out of the top of my boots, and Don is drenched. His teeth chatter and he shakes like low voltage current is passing through him.

Matt helps us to the bank. "Keep moving to get the body heat pumping." He reaches into his pack, unscrewing the cup from a thermos and fills it halfway before handing it to Don. Steam hovers over the cup. Digging deep in his pack, Matt produces a wool stocking cap. He hands it to Don who pulls it over his wet, matted hair. Matt looks at me and does a quick triage assessment: "You're not that wet so you can help find wood."

Don stomps around, drinking and eating a chocolate bar to stay warm while Matt and I search every sheltered tree crook and trunk cavity in the area for anything burnable. Matt rummages through his pack again and yanks out a Ziploc bag with a lighter, candle, and a can of dried spruce sap—instant fire starter. A large pile of branches is gathered, and Matt uses the candle to ignite the spruce sap. It burns hot and steady as we place branches on the growing flames. Don is practically standing over the fire, not wanting to miss one BTU, smoke curling around him and steam rising from his wet clothing. I sit on a damp log, boots off and the wrung-out socks so close to the fire I smell singed wool. Staring at my prune-like toes, the warmth from the fire creeps back into them.

Matt peers at his watch after fifteen minutes. "Time to go."

Nobody wants to leave the comfort of the fire but there is no choice—it's bad enough to spend the night in the woods, but to do it with wet clothes on a frosty night pushes the hazard meter in my head to "red" level. Only the rushing stream makes any sound. We kick the remains of the fire, grind it out with our boots and head to the tree Don fell from crossing the creek.

"I'll go first," Matt says. "Monty, want me to carry the rifle across the creek?"

I'm offended Matt isn't confident I can pack the rifle across the creek. I've lugged the gun all over the woods for weeks and in a weird way, bonded with it and all the forms a rifle is carried: cradle, shoulder, one-handed, two-handed, sling, and everything in-between. "I can handle it."

"Suit yourself." Matt is on the horizontal tree, moving gingerly from limb to limb, probing for any loose bark.

Don follows and steps past the spot that sent him into the creek, looking relieved when he touches the far bank. I sling the rifle around my neck and stare ahead at each limb, careful not to get mesmerized with the creek hurtling past below me.

When we are all across, Don hands me a candy bar.

"I don't know how long I'd be in spin cycle if you didn't pluck me out."

Matt raises his eyebrows to acknowledge a rare moment; humility and contrition from Don are not qualities in large supply. This is the closest we might get to an admission of fallibility. I drink it in and savor it. Matt stands stiffly. "Probably time to push ahead. Let's hope the rest of this bushwhack is less eventful."

Once we climb out of the ravine, the terrain flattens and light filters through the woods. "Thank God," I say. "I see the beach."

"Well, it's about time," Don says. "Three hours of hell."

Matt checks his watch. "It's 5:00 p.m. and the tide is coming in."

If we don't move fast, the tide will push us right into the trees where the walking is much slower than on the beach.

I'm fifty yards ahead, walking steadily, my mind toggling between the blister erupting on my heel and the rifle sling chafing my shoulder. The allure of such a beautiful place is replaced with fatigue and the dampness from my clinging, sweaty clothes. It doesn't take long for Matt and Don to catch me. We keep one eye on the approaching tide and the other on the rocks and sand in front of us.

We need to travel a long arc of shoreline, cross a rocky point, then angle along the beach for another half-mile before we are at camp. At this time of the year, it gets dark early, too. The forced march continues at a pace somewhere between a brisk walk and a half-trot. The threat of hypothermia held at bay—momentarily—by our rapid pace. We cross the treeless prominence and see water lapping at the rocks just below us.

Don breaks the quiet. "I just want a big, juicy steak tonight."

Nobody answers.

"What about you?" Don asks.

"I'll eat anything they put in front of me," I say.

Matt chimes in, "I'm with you there."

Soon we are back on the beach, tide at our heels. We slosh through the water in our rubber boots as long as possible before it gets too deep and then move off the gravel and rock into the beach grass—our last haven before re-entering the darkening woods. The water edges into the grass with the tide and we plunge across a small creek.

The radio surprises us: "Dickens, this is Gilbert Bay, over." It's a reminder that there are other people in this world, in this bay, and the comfort of camp is not far away after our grueling hike.

Matt forages in his pack and pulls out the radio. "This is Dickens, go ahead Gilbert Bay."

"The helicopter is fixed but it's too dark to fly now. What's your location?"

"We're just north of camp."

"Okay, shouldn't be too long before we see you," Walt says. "I've set out a lantern on the big rock in front of camp to guide you."

"Much appreciated."

"Tell them we want steak!" Don says.

"I've got a pretty hungry crew here. Hope dinner's ready."

"Dinner will be waiting. See you in a bit. Gilbert Bay out."

"You should have told them we want steak," Don adds.

The tide pushes us into the narrow space between the scrum of alder marking the beginning of the woods and the last of the tall beach grass. The grass hides logs and chunks of driftwood half-buried in sand. In the diminished light it's a minefield we pick our way through, half by sight, half by feel. We cross a small spit with a copse of young spruce trees and see the lantern not far in the distance.

Our pace quickens once again and Don bustles ahead of us.

"Take it easy or you'll break a leg before you make it to camp," Matt cautions.

"But I'm God-damn starving," Don says.

We stumble through the dusk for another few minutes, the ground turns sandy, our footing improves, and then the scent of a barbecue hits us. Don runs full speed and disappears into the clearing at camp.

Matt's disembodied form in the fading light says, "Race you to camp?"

It's a nutty thing to do but maybe Don inspired a little crazy in us. The twin horsemen of fatigue and hunger do their job. "You're on."

The lantern is a charged speck in the distance as we race off in its direction, our arms windmilling, raincoats flapping, packs bouncing on our backs, as graceful as two charging water buffalo.

Collapsing on the ground and laughing in the flicker of light we gasp for breath. A side of Matt reveals itself as subtle as a window curtain slowly parting. I no longer feel the nagging blister on my heel or my boulder-heavy thighs. For me, at this moment, we are truly a crew—and for once, I am part of it.

And I smell steak.

NED THAYER – OUTDOORSMAN

The doorbell rang and Ned crutched his way from the sofa, past the granite-countered kitchen island and into the hallway of his Aspen condo. Before he could get to the door, the bell rang again.

"Coming, coming." Ned was not used to moving at the speed of a sloth. Four days ago, his ingrown, left big toenail was reduced in size by one-third. Red streaks now laced their way past his ankle, hot with infection.

Earlier in the day, Doc Sorensen stopped by with unsettling news. "Aside from removing more nail than usual, the infection worries me more. You need to be off your feet for at least a week or that blood poisoning is going to move up your leg. I want you lying down with your leg up—one week minimum—got it?"

Stay off his feet? Ned never stopped moving. His constitution was legendary. In fact, he couldn't remember the last time he had a cold. He splinted his own leg after a climbing accident in the Karakoram (an orthopedist later said he'd never examined a better set tibia), and sewn half his ear back on with dental floss after flipping his raft and cracking his head on a first descent of the Zambezi River.

Ned made a living ignoring doctor's orders but this was different. His feet were insured with Lloyd's of London, and nothing was too good for him. After all, he was the moneymaking machine of the outdoor adventure world. Everyone wanted to be like Ned. Need a new route on a seamless pitch of dark granite? He would wear your company's new climbing line. Kayak the North Sea in January? Ned would do it while he modeled your state-of-the-art dry suit.

Leaning on his crutches, he opened the door.

"Hi Ned, sorry to drop in on you unannounced but I am in town for business and thought it would be good to talk face-to-face."

"Sasha, good to see you." Not really. He smiled at his ex-wife, wondering what she planned on extracting from him this time.

Ned hadn't always felt like this. He had squired lots of women, but only one had smitten him: Sasha Neiman.

* * *

She had almost run him over on the slopes at Sun Valley while he was telemark skiing. Ned brushed snow off himself.

"Are you okay?" Sasha said as she popped her goggles off. Ned wasn't hurt, but he leapt out of the way at the last minute to avoid having her ski tips disappear into his chest. "I guess I was a bit out of control," Sasha admitted.

He wanted to say, "No shit, you were totally airborne where two runs converge." Instead, Ned offered, "I'm still in one piece. I should pay more attention."

"I'll make it up to you," she offered. "Let's finish the run together and I'll buy you a beer."

"Can't argue with that," Ned agreed.

Despite all the accolades and accomplishments, a hole existed in Ned's life: a human connection. His friendships consisted of jamming his feet into his climbing partner's armpits to ward off frostbite, slamming frosty beers down with buddies at a remote way station, or rollicking under the sheets with some sinewy siren. Ned thought Sasha was the missing piece.

* * *

"Can I come in, it's freezing out here," Sasha said.

"Oh sure, sorry."

"What happened to you, Ned?"

"I'm felled by an ingrown toenail and infection of all things," Ned said.

"I guess you are mortal," Sasha said. "Before I forget, Savannah wanted me to give you this." Sasha reached into her pocket and handed Ned a worn tennis ball.

Savannah was the joint custody product of their ex-marriage. Ned adored his daughter, but his lifestyle didn't make it easy to be a dad.

"Savannah's in town with friends right now, but she wants to come over while she's here to play 'roll-y ball.'"

Ned and Savannah liked to sit on the floor and roll the ball down the hallway to each other. "Roll-y ball sounds fun but Daddy's laid up." Ned set the ball on the sofa end table. "I'm supposed be in bed for a week. It's killing me."

"Go lay down and I'll pull up a chair. Do you have a few minutes?"

Oh, oh. Ned wasn't sure he liked where this was heading. He lay prone on the couch, an Eddie Bauer down quilt draped over him. "I've got plenty of time right now."

"As you know, I still have our old condo on Black Diamond Street." Sasha draped her down jacket over a dark leather chair. "There are renters in it now and I'm gonna be doing some remodeling. I'm still in the planning phase: looking for tile, plumbing fixtures, countertops, and getting contractors lined up. Plus, I still sit on the board of the ski area, so I have some work to do with them."

Ned sensed there was more than business on this visit.

"Look Ned, I know the last few months have been tough."

For the first time since the divorce, Sasha was softening.

"Ned, what happened to us? I've gone over it in my head and I can't trace where the problems started." She touched her temple, as if that might release a hidden answer.

"I think it goes all the way back to Kitzbuhl," Ned said.

"Why Kitzbuhl?"

Ned wasn't sure how much detail to include fearing it might unleash the Sasha Beast.

* * *

He had watched Sasha ski off a small rock face—a routine jump by her standards—and land with both legs hyperextended. Her anterior cruciate ligaments snapped louder than frost pockets in a maple tree on a subzero night. In seconds, he was beside her as she thrashed in the snow.

"What the hell happened? Are you okay?" Ned asked.

"They're gone," she moaned. "My knees—I think I blew 'em out."

"Both of them?" Ned was incredulous. He could understand one knee and a broken collarbone or dislocated shoulder, but two knees—that's hard to do. He bent over and started unzipping the legs of her ski pants.

She shrieked, "What are you doing!?"

"Sash, I gotta check your legs."

"All right, but be careful."

Sure enough, any trace of the kneecaps had disappeared in a mass of swollen flesh. Sasha's knees looked like they were replaced by cantaloupes.

"What do you think?" Sasha asked.

In his best bedside manner Ned offered, "I think your knees are trashed. Look, Sash, I've got to get help. I'm going to have to leave you for a bit while I find the ski patrol. I'll be back as soon as I can."

The ski patrol strapped her into the litter and Ned looked at his wife. She was quiet with a sedated expression—the face of surrender. He'd observed that look on too many friends who had never made it out of the hills. Two blown-out knees wouldn't kill her, but he was surprised by her docile reaction—no anger, frustration, or pouting.

Surgery and eight months of physical therapy had Sasha's knees functioning again. Not everything else was.

* * *

Sasha shifted her chair closer to Ned. "Are you saying I lost my edge after Kitzbuhl?"

Ned treaded carefully around his answer. "It kinda marked a shift, if you want to call it that."

"Because I wanted to start a family?"

Ned thought of Skittles, their golden retriever, who now resided with Sasha and was not part of the joint custody agreement. "We had a family—me, you and Skittles."

"C'mon, Ned. I was thirty-four. The clock was ticking."

Why did that clock always sound like Big Ben to Ned? Twelve months later it chimed, and Savannah Selway Thayer was born. Ned managed to be there for the birth, but missed her first and third birthdays. He did sing "Happy Birthday" via satellite phone. By Ned's calculations, he missed 821 days out of the 1,460 days Savannah was alive. "Maybe I wasn't ready for kids yet."

"Ned, you're forty-two now. When, if ever, did you think you'd be ready for kids? How long do you think you can keep this up?"

Ouch. This was a tender spot for Ned: his legacy. The aches lingered, his reflexes a millisecond slower. He relied on the "Ned Team" to keep him in top form: Bruno, his massage therapist, who pummeled every muscle and tendon in his body, Irene (dietician/cook), Karin (rolfer), Sami (yoga guru), Wanda (sports psychologist), and a host of others to fend off the youngsters creeping up on him, putting him to the test. "Don't worry, the afterburners still can kick in when I need them."

Sasha propped a leg up on the sofa. "I don't know Ned; I think you're kidding yourself. I saw you on TV last year in the Aussie Foreplay and you looked tapped out."

Sasha had a keen eye. In Australia, he polished off the marathon run across a mountain range, shredded a headwind on the bike ride across a bleak desert plain, and plowed a wake on the two-mile swim up a river. He almost ran out of gas in the last event, the five-mile sack race. Those Aussies and their sense of humor! His lead was so big his final pathetic hops to the finish line were not noticed by the press. Was this the beginning of the end? Was he going to wind up doing car commercials or hosting a low-rated cable TV program?

"And what about those youngsters nipping at your heels? How in the world will you keep up with Krupp? He's an animal."

Ned shared Sasha's assessment of Krupp Condor, the legendary mountaineer from Bavaria. He made his hometown of Zugspitze-Strassen-Hossel a household word. Physically a monster, with semi-Neanderthal features, Krupp had no peer where power was required. He scaled all the toughest peaks without oxygen or climbing support and his rescue of three Japanese climbers during an ascent of Habu Dal's west face made international news. Krupp's English was good with enough German accent to catch the ear of the American market. "You know Sasha, it's a mental game too. I may not be twenty-five anymore, but I know all the tricks and have a lot more experience."

"It's not always about what's between your ears, Ned, and you know it. To be a player, you need the best expeditions, but the trendsetters also have another ingredient: *joie de vivre*, charisma, a certain charm. You have it, but maybe people have Ned-fatigue and want a bright, shiny new star." Sasha paused, went to the fridge, grabbed a sports drink, and sat down.

"Help yourself," Ned said. "I'd get up and cook but this toe thing—"

"Ha, ha! You cook now? When did that start? Anyway, I know your Q Rating is down a notch and that *chica*, whatever her name is, and sprawled all over the *Sports Illustrated* swimsuit issue, is on the rise."

"You mean Heidi?"

"Yeah, that's her name."

Heidi McCarrins was another tough tripwire. Ned saw the trend: women edging in on a men's club. An attractive and ferocious competitor with crossover appeal to both men and women, she made her name in water sports. Surfing, kayaking, and windsailing were her specialties. The thong bikini hadn't hurt her exposure either. Two big splashes pushed her to a new level. The hundred-mile ride of a tsunami wave in the Tasmanian Sea was incredible. More amazing was her sudden appearance on the U.S. Women's Olympic ice hockey team. Her bone-crushing check on the Canadian captain got replayed on TVs across the world. Shit, where did she learn how to skate, anyway?

"And we can't forget Reid, either." Sasha had left her boots at the door and rubbed her SmartWool-clad feet together. "He's always a wild card. He's a bit younger than you, but he doesn't have the wear and tear because he does fewer trips."

Reid Robinson emerged periodically from a Kaczynski-like cabin in Montana and pulled off audacious trips to obscure parts of the world. It might be a hot air balloon trip across South America or the first sand-ski across the Sahara. He'd then retreat to his warren, reappearing across the globe eight months later. Reid was the J.D. Salinger of his sport. There were occasional sightings of him buying groceries or working at his friend's ranch—Lloyd Carver, the Zoom Power Bar magnate. With Lloyd's backing, Reid had no need for other sponsors. The public gobbled up Reid's anti-corporate, renegade approach to the business. *Outside Magazine* deified the guy in its article, "The Last Man Standing: Reid Robinson at the Summit."

"So where are you going with this, Sash?" Ned asked.

"I want you to be a bigger part of Savannah's life. I don't want to exclude you. And I want her to have a live dad, not a dead one. I'm afraid you're going to come home from a trip in a box—if they manage to find your body."

"Sash, we've gone over this a hundred times. Don't you think you're worrying too much?"

Sasha got up and moved over to the stairwell wall near a collection of photos. "Really? How many of your friends—good friends—are dead? This is the Wall of the Dead."

No point arguing the numbers. Global adventurers with AARP cards were a rare breed. At least half a dozen friends had died on trips with Ned and a few on other people's trips. The first was the hardest. His college roommate, Steve, was swept over a precipice by an avalanche in the Canadian Rockies. He did a quick tally: Ben (snakebite in India), Sue (infection in Borneo), Mike (collision with snowboarder on Mount Blanc), Sirgay (disappeared at 27,000 feet in a Himalayan whiteout), Claude (impaled on sweeper, kayaking in the Hindu Kush), and Ryan (hit by bus in Addis Ababa).

"I made a good living—we made a good living." Ned was awash in money and business offers after his appearance on the cover of *Newsweek*. Sasha managed his business and had a real knack for it too. Ned wasn't hawking power tools or neon-colored electrolyte drinks. She lined up high-profile trips with first ascents and descents. He didn't do trips with egomaniacs, muscle-heads or the pay-per-climb crowd either. Top-notch sponsors provided the firepower, and didn't push him to attend outdoor gear conventions and do promotional videos. Ned and Sasha bought a ranch in Sun Valley. Life was bountiful and the responsibilities minimal. He worked damn hard, liked what he did, and provided for his family. Couldn't she understand? "I feel like we're rehashing the same arguments we used to have."

Ned had called this the mogul phase of their marriage. Counseling came first, trailed by anger, lawyers, separation, and divorce—all within the tidy span of ten months. One thing he always admired about Sasha: once she pointed the car in the direction she wanted to go, the engine was gunned. Or maybe it was a bulldozer flattening him.

Ned hated fussing about money the most. He never got into this business for the money; it was the sense of freedom, the smell of pine trees, and the sun-drenched warmth of a rock face. The intoxicating blend of mind and body pushed to the maximum, fighting fierce challenges from the best athletes in the world. The mad rush of adrenaline.

The money made it easier to do bigger, more ambitious trips, eat at better restaurants, and drive more powerful cars. As long as there was enough cash, he didn't care how much there was, and he didn't want to bog down in the details. Nobody was surprised when Sasha did. Her meticulous nature made every negotiation over bank accounts, financial statements, and real estate holdings a numerical form of torture.

"I know you're not happy about me getting half of everything," Sasha said. "Don't forget I worked my ass off for six years."

It was pointless to add that she might be running a ski lift right now if the business wasn't Ned Thayer, Inc.

Ned noticed Sasha getting worked up. She stood and took the empty plastic sports drink container over to the counter.

"Where's your recycling?"

"Under the counter to your left."

Sasha dropped the bottle in the bin. "There's one more thing. I want to invite you for Savannah's birthday at the end of March. I'd like it to be special."

Ned peered at the calendar on the wall. It was a Ned Thayer First Ascents calendar with some damn fine shots of Ned, either shirtless while dangling off a rock wall, or covered head to toe in Gore Tex with rime ice clinging to his face. "Sure, I can do it. It's four months away. Sounds like fun."

"Great, I'll get back to you with the details. Maybe we can talk again tomorrow after my meeting."

"It's just me and my toe—I'm not going anywhere. I hope you don't mind if I don't see you out."

Ned had barely processed Sasha's visit when the cell phone rang. Randy, Ned's agent, was on the line. "Hey, it's my daily check in." Randy's keyboard clattered in the background. "The North Face is concerned about your toe and wants to know your availability for next fall's catalogue. There's a bigger problem, though. They want to be cutting edge, and they're looking to go younger, fresher." Randy paused to let that sink in. "I got the feeling they think you're dimming. They are a hair away from signing Heidi to replace you. Maybe you can come up with a kick-ass adventure that will wow the world. Hey, I got a call I gotta take. See ya."

Ned settled back on the bed. Now what? It pissed him off The North Face was ready to discard him like a rusting piece of machinery—after fourteen years! —right out of their sponsorship. He was not immune to introspection although those moments often came while he was in motion. Or after sex with some hard-bodied climbing hottie. Ned cracked open a bottle of herbal-infused tea parked on the end table and took a few swigs. In his mind, he knew Sasha was right; he couldn't keep going at this pace. At some point, he was going to embarrass himself.

Ned gave himself two or three more years before he'd lose the edge. The mind was keen, but the body had a lot of miles on it. The gnawing question crept in: How much money did he need? He was wealthy beyond any ski bum's dreams, well-connected from Wall Street to the big walls of Yosemite, and had friends on every continent.

Ned hobbled to the kitchen, so hungry he ripped the box for a burrito with his mouth. As he watched the burrito spin inside the microwave, his mind drifted, and Ned wondered how it would all end for him. A simple epitaph etched on a granite tombstone: Ned Thayer, Outdoorsman. It had a nice ring to it. The words from his friend Bjorn, the Norwegian dog sled champion who had crossed Greenland in a month-long whiteout, came back to him, "Think about death, give up on life." He wasn't exactly sure what Bjorn meant but it had to do with hanging up the old climbing harness. Bjorn wasn't around to clarify either; only his lead dog had survived the trek across Greenland.

The phone rang again. *Can't get a minute's peace around here.* Ned stared at the unfamiliar number on the phone's display. "Hello?"

"Hello? Is dis Ned Tayer?"

"Yes, this is Ned."

"Hello, Ned, this is Petr. Petr Saminovich. Vee meet in de Himalayas two years ago. Do you remember? I never drink so much chang in my life!"

"What a killer night, from what I remember of it. It's awesome to hear from you." Wow, Petr Saminovich. This guy was the best all-around climber in the world. Ice. Rock. The whole package—he did it all.

"I've got a wild idea," Petr gushed.

"Have you been drinking more chang?"

"No, no, I sober—at least right now. Ha, ha! Listen to dis. I vanted to do somting very deeferent. Den it come to me: the Cirque of the Unclimbables on Baffin Island. Vee could do it—you and me! Or vee die trying. Ha, ha! I got it all set up, everyting is go. You say yes and show up. Leave de rest to me. If vee pull dis off, vee two world famous guys. But it has to happen end of March when I have climbing permit. I also am booked rest of year. If you can't do it, I try Krupp Condor. Krupp is a machine! But he's German and vee Russians have de grudge. So, I peek you first! Vat do you say?"

The Cirque of the Unclimbables—in March no less. Getting to base camp would be a survival test. Gale force winds with a chill cutting like a stiletto and whiteouts making bathroom stops a life-or-death enterprise. Five thousand feet of vertical granite on every face, each colder than a morgue slab. It was bold, stupid, suicidal, and totally intriguing. No doubt anyone who nailed the last great mountaineering challenge would be mentioned in the same breath with Sir Edmund Hillary. Petr was the right guy to pull it off. He was rock-solid and thorough in his trip planning and calculation of risk. Petr could bring his mother back alive from this trip. If Petr believed he'd pull it off, it was as good as done. The very idea of Krupp Condor replacing him on this climb sent a shudder down to Ned's big toe. He'd show The North Face and the other doubters!

"I'm in."

"Good, very, very good," said Petr. "I knew I count on you. I geev call back in a few days, we work out details."

Ned flashed to his dicey climbs. You could always turn back like many of the others did, but the magic was in trying to find that fine line. But trying didn't mean dying—Ned enjoyed life too much to do stupid stuff. Had he cheated death before? Certainly. The difference between bad luck and bad judgment was a blur or a blink of an eye. Like railroad tracks running to the horizon, he didn't want to find where those two lines converged. This was going to work; everything pointed to the time being right.

The little matter of a conflict with Savannah's birthday party needed sorting out. Ned could make a blazing fire out of yak dung within minutes or fashion a raft out of goat bladders, but tough social situations always proved to be a conundrum. Breaking the news to Sasha about another missed birthday was rougher than any climb with Petr. This was gonna take just the right personal touch. Ned raked over options on tone, delivery, wording, and then the right words came together. Like a rock face's secrets revealing themselves, inviting Ned to ascend.

Ned grabbed the tennis ball from the end table. He was going to need a grip of steel to conquer the Cirque and he squeezed it so many times, beads of sweat seeped out of every pore on his head. Images of Savannah struggling to get off the ski lift last year, hitting a piñata on her birthday, and chasing Skittles filled his head. After a half hour of stringing long-ignored memories, along with a burning in his forearms and hands, he realized he'd made the right decision.

Sasha arrived with Savannah the next day. Savannah's pink snow suit matched the glow in her cheeks. She ran to Ned and landed on him reclining on the sofa.

Ned tickled her. "I didn't know you were so fast."

"I'm bigger now," Savannah said.

"So, I see."

Sasha dropped Savannah's backpack on the floor. "I've got to run out for a while so I'm going to leave you two alone."

"Hold on a sec." Ned crutched to an upright position. "I need to talk with you."

Sasha's eyebrows shot up like little antennas. "About?"

"Savannah, could you do mommy and daddy a favor?" Ned handed her his iPad from the end table. "Take this in the bedroom and play those cartoons you like so much. Mommy and Daddy have to talk for a bit."

Sasha stood, arms crossed, ready for trench warfare. "Well?"

"It's about Savannah's birthday." No matter how many times Ned practiced in his mind the best way to say things, he never was sure how it was going to spew out.

"You're bailing, right?" Sasha's face looked like a thunderstorm sweeping in.

"Well, kind of—"

"Jesus, Ned. You're either in or out. Which is it?"

"Both."

Sasha put her hand on her forehead, wandered into the kitchen. Taking a deep breath, she drew her hand over her face with such force it looked like it would rub off. "This better be good."

"I'm going with Petr Saminovich to the Cirque of the Unclimbables." Ned crutched into the kitchen and faced Sasha. "We're gonna summit all of them. It will be awesome." Ned pictured he and Petr drinking slushy champagne back in camp while their feet thawed.

"What about Savannah's birthday?"

"You better sit down."

Sasha parked herself on a breakfast bar stool.

"I'm retiring after the Cirque. Going out on top." He was giddy with the certainty of his decision. A light-headedness, like oxygen deprivation at altitude, swept over him. "I want to be a bigger part of Savannah's life."

Sasha cocked her head and stared at him for a second, "You're serious, aren't you?"

"Yup." He walked over to the Wall of the Dead and started taking down the photos of his departed friends.

"What are you doing?"

"Moving on. You were right—much as I hate to admit it. I'm aging out. I can take it down a notch and still have fun. Only I'm gonna do it with Savannah."

"Can I get it in writing?" she asked.

"Sasha." Ned wavered. "Everything about our divorce has been in writing, packed with legalese. I hate that shit. This is going to be a handshake." He stuck his hand out.

Sasha paused before shaking it. "Okay, I'm going to take off. I'll pick Savannah up in about two hours." She gathered her pocketbook near the door. "Please don't tell me you've changed your mind when I come back."

"Savannah!" Ned yelled. "Wanna play roll-y ball?"

She shot out of the bedroom, tossed the iPad on the sofa, and sat at one end of the hallway, legs splayed out in front of her.

"I thought you had to have your leg up?" Sasha said.

"A little roll-y ball won't kill me."

They sat at each end of the hallway, the ball rocketing back and forth between them. Ned watched Savannah's lightning reflexes—for a four-year-old!—and saw his future. He'll load up the van with skis, bikes, climbing gear, kayaks, and Bun-Bun, Savannah's favorite stuffed animal. They'll shoot the wildest rivers, ski the deepest powder, trek the tallest mountains—together! Ned is all in! She'll be on the cover of Outside by the time she's fifteen. Move over Heidi McCarrins. Savannah Selway Thayer is right behind you.

PALM SUNDAY

I'm eating breakfast in the dining hall seated next to Harry when the screen door bangs open. Marlon, the Camp High Pines swimming counselor, saunters over in his customary outfit of flip flops, white Red Cross lifeguard trunks, and a tank top. His arms wrap around our shoulders, biceps squeezing like a python coiling. Vapor from his Head and Shoulders shampoo thickens the air.

"Well guys, how are you going to do on Palm Sunday? Anyone wanna make a prediction?"

I stop cutting a rubbery pancake. "What's a good take for the weekend?"

"Three to four hundred bucks, depending on how generous the parents are and how much you suck up to them." He leers and adds, "Brian, you'll never see that kind of money for tying trees together with twine." Marlon leans over, grabs a sausage from my plate, and gulps it down.

As the campcraft counselor, I've spent the previous four weeks teaching knot-tying, fire-building, and lean-to construction to kids who are too nerdy, bored, or uncoordinated to play in the fiercely competitive camp sports. I take special satisfaction at the kids who discover the unforgiving precision of a knot and the promise of a crackling-dry pile of kindling.

Marlon repeats the question: "Anyone wanna make a prediction?" He looks directly at me.

Blood rushes to my face, and I turn from the table to face Marlon. "I don't see how you'll manage to pull it off since all you do is sit on your ass with a pith helmet on, rubbing Coppertone on your shoulders."

Marlon's real name is Dan Bickett, but I had dubbed him "Marlon" after Marlon Brando from *On the Waterfront*. From the top of his lifeguard stand, Marlon's voice always booms, "there's no running on the waterfront," or "don't dunk on the waterfront." The nickname stuck like a turd to a shoe. Even though Marlon bestowed memorable nicknames, he didn't think it fair for him to have one, particularly when it came from me, a rookie counselor.

Marlon takes a step back and stands for a second or two, like he's studying his prey before striking. "Look who's strutting his stuff—the new guy from Joisey. You're so funny you should be in the Sunday comics." Marlon pauses for emphasis. "I'll bet you fifty bucks I double whatever you get."

The camp's caste system had counselors who were former kids at camp at the top of the pecking order. Marlon's one of them—like frat boys at rush season. "Hey Brian, get me a cup of coffee." "Hey Brian, take my dishes back to the kitchen." In their eyes, I hadn't paid my dues yet or shown the proper measure of respect to the camp's old guard who defended the New Hampshire camp's fifty-year-old traditions as if they were Freemason rituals. I'll be damned if I'm gonna kiss spoiled kids' asses. I left their dishes where they were. My back had a target on it and Marlon wanted to plunge a knife in it.

Marlon heads to the door, and I shout, "You're on!"

KEN POST · 109

Without looking back, Marlon says, "We'll settle after taps."

Harry slumps in his chair. "I think you lost fifty bucks. You could have bought me a lot of beer with that money."

"C'mon Harry, let's get out of here." I push my plate away and head for the door.

I trudge back to my cabin by the lake's edge and flop on my bunk. This summer, the kids in my cabin are known affectionately as "The Swamp Rats." I enjoy the Rats, despite the challenging age between zits and driver's license learner permits. Most of their parents are bank presidents, stockbrokers, airline executives, doctors, and lawyers. The expensive cars, new tennis racquets, and shiny golf clubs are a chasm between these affluent kids and anything I experienced in suburban New Jersey.

I grab *Time Magazine* from my trunk under the steel-frame bunk bed and sit on the porch. Engrossed in an article about Gerry Ford running for president, I barely notice the gray Mercedes pull up near my cabin. Out steps Randy Veracci, one of my Rats, and his dad, a big, athletic man with a dark tan and a blazing white tennis outfit.

Randy does the introductions: "Dad, I'd like you to meet Brian, he's the leader of the Swamp Rats I told you about. I'll be back in a minute; I have to grab my glove in the cabin."

"Swamp Rats, eh? Sounds like a bunch of rebels. Hi, I'm Mike Veracci." A giant hand extends with a class ring the size of a golf ball. "Randy's told me a lot about you and says he's having one helluva summer and thinks the world of you." Mr. Veracci looks over his shoulder to see if Randy is within earshot and lowers his voice. "Randy didn't have a great time here last year and wasn't sure he wanted to come back. We kind of pressured him to give it another shot so we're really glad it worked out."

We exchange pleasantries for a few minutes. Randy previously filled me in about his dad and the tipping scenario about to play out. This is not uncommon; a lot of kids know how much the tip will be, right down to the delivery, and passed it on. If a kid is a jerk, the tip is held over your head for special treatment or privileges.

"C'mon down to the car, I want to show you something," says Mike. This is the big moment. Mike pops the trunk filled with baseball gloves, tennis racquets, footballs, and golf clubs. "Take your pick of anything you want. It's how I say thanks." Mike beams as if Blackbeard's treasure chest opened.

"Wow, Mr. Veracci. The truth is, I'm pretty well-stocked with athletic gear." Randy told me his dad first offered the gear but came up with cash as a follow up. The trick was to tactfully "hold out" so you didn't offend his dad. He'd mention money, up to thirty dollars if he liked you.

"Sure, sure," Mike says. "A guy in good shape like you would have all his own stuff. I should have suspected that. Let's make this easy." Mike reaches for his wallet and three crisp tens are in his left hand. The right hand is for the handshake, like when I got my high school diploma the previous year.

"Mr. Veracci, this is very generous."

"No problem, you college guys need all the help you can get. Hey, if I were you, I'd use it to let off a little steam in Hanover." Mike cups his hands to his mouth and shouts to Randy, "What's going on in there? Are you ready to have brunch with your mom and sister?"

Randy emerges from the cabin with a nice blue Wilson tennis shirt on and his baseball glove.

"Let's go. Your mom is probably wondering what happened to us. Brian, really nice meeting you." Randy jumps in the passenger seat and gives me the thumbs-up as the car pulls out. I fold the three tens into my wallet and can't believe my luck.

About an hour later while I'm sweeping the cabin, Joey, aka "Gonzo" Garuba's parents wander down the hill in their tennis outfits with racquets under their arms. Mr. Garuba has big sweat stains under his armpits, and his pockets are stuffed with tennis balls. Mrs. Garuba pats her forehead with a Kleenex. I meet them on the steps.

"Hello, Mr. and Mrs. Garuba. Pretty hot out there today, huh?" I set the broom down on the porch. "You guys are brave to take on this heat with a game of tennis. Why don't we stop by the dining hall and track down a drink to cool you off."

"Thank you, Brian, that's a good idea," says Mrs. G.

Ten minutes and three Cokes later, I sense Mr. G moving in for the kill. "So, how's Joey doing this summer anyway? He says he loves every minute of it."

"I'm glad he's having a good time here," I say.

"I'd like to give you a token of our appreciation. You know, a little help with your college money." He pulls out his wallet and scans the bills for a minute. "Honey, I don't have any smaller bills here. Would you run up to the car and grab your purse?"

"Sure." Mrs. G sets her Coke down on the bench. "Don't forget, I'm gonna put this on your tab. You already owe me twenty bucks from our tennis match."

A few minutes later she is back with the purse and produces twenty dollars. I thank them, and they head up the hill where their car is parked.

The rest of the morning passes uneventfully with the other four parents all wandering by with their own version of uncomfortable small talk, or genuinely friendly chatter and curiosity about their kid's summer, before eventually tipping me. Willie's dad, Mr. Berger, owns a large landscaping business, and seems embarrassed when he hands me the tip. The twenty-dollar bill is neatly folded in Mr. Berger's pocket, deftly transferred to his hand, and wedged between his index and middle fingers. As we shake hands, the bill appears in my palm like an illicit deal going down.

My take for the day is 135 dollars, and I make a mental note to keep fifty bucks separate to pay Marlon at taps. In the dining hall at lunch the counselors compare notes. Harry is the surprise of the weekend so far with 200 dollars. Marlon drops his tray off near the kitchen and spots me. He pulls his wallet out and fans the bills in his hand like a peacock spreading his tail. The rumor is Marlon made 380 dollars.

The afternoon burns clear and hot, and the deserted camp possesses a peculiar calm in place of the unharnessed energy normally pulsating into every corner of it. The remainder of the day figures to be slow since I've already received tips from all the parents of kids in my cabin.

I wander up the hill from the lake toward my campcraft area, and cut into the woods on a well-worn path where a gray clapboard shed sits off to side of a small open spot in the pines and birches. The clearing has an assemblage of pitched lean-to's, camp furniture, and fire rings.

KEN POST · 113

I spin the combination lock until it clicks open, and step inside where light enters the shed sparingly from a single four-pane window in the back. The musty smell of canvas tarps, mingled with the blend of wood smoke, soil, and Coleman fuel always gives me a special comfort. I plan to sort gear for the wilderness trip I'm setting up with several of my prize pupils on the remote western shore of Lake Meguntic. As I pull a list from my pocket, a branch snaps—someone is coming down the trail.

Stepping outside, I'm surprised to see Jon Algernon and his parents approaching.

"Hello," I say.

"Good afternoon," replies the woman. "We stopped at your cabin but you weren't there. Jon suggested we look here. Excuse me, I should introduce myself. I'm Jon's mom, Susan," she says as we shake hands. Her hand is thin and fragile and she's wearing a white tennis skirt and pink top, with brown hair tied back. "This is Bill, he's a friend of mine," she says, motioning to the man I thought was Jon's father. Bill remains several feet back smoking a cigarette while leaning against a white pine. He smiles slightly and nods when introduced but does not move forward to shake hands. Bill is slight with an angular face and close-cropped hair with a touch of gray hair around his temples.

"We're sorry to bother you this afternoon," Mrs. Algernon says. "We planned to stop by yesterday but got so caught up with things in Hanover we didn't make it." She brushes a stray hair out of her face. "Jon really wanted to come so we made a point of getting an early start today. I hope we haven't inconvenienced you."

"No, not at all, Mrs. Algernon."

"Please call me Susan. Jon wanted to show us what he learned here. That's why he was so anxious to come."

Jon is a quiet kid, almost somber, who doesn't have many friends at camp. His pale, dish-shaped face is often expressionless and reminds me of a barn owl. He isn't athletic and finds refuge at my little clearing in the woods. Since he doesn't talk much, I don't really know him well. Jon is a good listener, always willing to help out in camp, but whatever light is there stays shuttered deep inside him. In this special niche, Jon quietly goes about his work, carefully lashing logs and perfecting his bowline. I like Jon and sense in him a new and powerful confidence. Here in the woods, Jon is good at something, and I respect him because of the pride he takes in his work. Nothing has come easy to Jon like so many of the other wealthy kids at High Pines. He doesn't appear pampered, but wants to belong, to fit in.

I put my hand on Jon's shoulder and ask, "What did you want to show your mom?"

"He wants to make a campfire." Susan says. "Isn't that right?"

Jon nods. "Yeah."

"Okay, I'll get the matches out of the shed. You go get the kindling and wood."

"Don't forget," Jon adds, "the pot and the water."

"Oh yeah, thanks for reminding me."

I step from the shed with the pot and water and Jon has already deposited two small piles of fine kindling the thickness of pencil lead next to the campfire circle, and gone searching for more wood. Jon periodically squats, picks up a twig and adds it to his two-fisted collection.

KEN POST · 115

Jon's mom sits on a log; her eyes follow her son from point to point with a look of part amusement and part astonishment. Bill periodically looks at his watch.

Jon comes back to the fire ring and leaves several more bundles of kindling, all arranged in small piles arrayed from fine white pine twigs to small branches.

"My, how meticulous, Jon," Mrs. Algernon says. "Honey, are all those piles necessary?"

"That's what I'm thinking too," Bill says. "How much wood do you need? Let's get on with show."

Jon sits on his haunches near the fire ring. He slowly swivels his head toward Bill. A moment passes and Jon says, "You can't rush building a fire. I get one match. One. After it gets started, I need all the wood to keep it going on its own. I can't afford to have the fire go out while I'm looking for firewood. You know, it not as simple as lighting a match."

"Okay, okay, son. I didn't know this was so scientific."

An uneasy silence descends, and the only sound is Jon cracking kindling.

"Take your time, hon," Mrs. Algernon says. She shoots an unkind glance back at Bill who shifts against the tree.

"I'm ready for my match now."

"Here ya go." I hand Jon a box of Blue Diamond Strike Anywhere matches.

Jon selects a match from the box, studies it a second and drags it along the well-worn striker pad on the side of the box. The match flares and burns almost up to Jon's fingertips before he drops it in the teepee of twigs. No smoke rises and Susan looks around anxiously. Jon kneels down and calmly blows on the fire. A flicker of red and a wisp of smoke curl out of the twigs. Jon gently places a few small branches on the developing pile of glowing embers and waits until it burns them before he adds more on the fire.

"Good job, son," Bill says. "That should do it, huh?"

"No," Jon responds. This time, Jon does not look at Bill and continues to add more wood on the fire, the pieces increasingly larger as the fire grows. "I have to boil the water."

The fire crackles and pops, and Jon sets the small black-ened pot with water directly on the thicker branches in the fire. Jon, on his haunches, covers the pot and everyone waits for the water to boil.

"So how is your summer going, Brian?" Mrs. Algernon asks.

"Oh, pretty good. It's been really hot though." The weather seems to be a safe subject.

"It looks like you have a nice, little spot here in the woods." Mrs. Algernon makes a sweeping motion with her hand in reference to the surrounding area.

"I like it because it's off the beaten path. One day this may all be Jon's."

"I'm not sure I understand," Mrs. Algernon says.

"What I mean is Jon seems to like it—you know the campcraft stuff. Maybe he'll wind up being a campcraft counselor someday."

"Oh, right. He does have a knack for it," Mrs. Algernon says. "I had no idea it was so complicated."

"It's not exactly rocket science, Susan," says Bill.

"There's more to it than I thought," Mrs. Algernon says.

"The water's boiling!" Puffs of steam push past the pot lid. Jon flicks the lid off with a stick to prove the water boiled.

"I'm impressed. What's next, honey?" Mrs. Algernon asks.

"I have to put the fire out, Mom."

"Oh, that's right. We can't leave it burning. Okay, you should do that."

"Why don't I go ahead and put the fire out and let you get on with your visit with your mom and Bill," I offer.

"If that's okay," Jon says.

"Sure, no problem."

"Well, that's very nice of you Brian," Mrs. Algernon says.

"Much appreciated," Bill says.

"Brian, it's a pleasure to meet you and thanks for giving Jon this opportunity." Mrs. Algernon offers her hand and we shake again. "Jon, why don't you and Bill head to the car and I'll be there in a bit. I want to catch up with Brian for a minute."

Bill turns his back to wander back down the trail and I notice his paisley shirt with a gob of pine sap stuck to it where he leaned on the tree. Serves that asshole right.

"That was great," Mrs. Algernon says.

"I'm glad you can see what Jon learned, Mrs. Algernon."

"Please call me Susan. To tell the truth—" She pauses for a second and looks back at the car— "it's an eventful Parents Weekend. You see, Jon is not a—" she searches for the right word— "he's not a confident boy. You probably noticed that. But today, when Jon made that fire, I saw how proud he was. The fire, and—oh, it's not just the fire. It's more than that. It's knots and other things, too. He's talked about stuff since yesterday. Things he's learned. He's not normally talkative. You probably noticed that, too. In fact, I have to drag things out of him. But not this weekend."

I think this is a good point to step in but I'm not sure what to say.

"I don't really know how to thank you. I realize you work with a lot of kids but he's one kid who learned more than anyone imagined." She stops as if she's waiting for the rest of her thoughts to catch up. "Listen to me, I'm rambling on like a crackpot. I'm not normally so expansive. Anyway, I'd like to do something for you."

She swings around a small leather pocket book from behind her. I hadn't noticed it because it slung over her shoulder attached to a thin strap.

"Look, Mrs. Alger—I mean Susan. You don't have to. It's part of my job."

She snaps her hand up with a surprising quickness, her palm facing my chest as if to deflect a speeding bullet. "It's too hot to debate and in any case, I insist. Please take this as my way of saying thanks." She unfolds a fifty-dollar bill and hands it to me.

"This is really generous."

Susan fishes in her pocketbook and hands me a business card: Susan Algernon, President, CREATIVE TALENT, New York City.

I look at the card, unfamiliar with the business.

"You may not know the company, but you've probably heard of a few of my clients: Meryl Streep, Robert De Niro, Al Pacino. If you ever need a reference, let me know. And if you ever find yourself in New York City, drop by—you never know who may be in the office and ready to autograph a photo for you."

I put the card in my wallet. "I had no idea. Thank you very much. I'm glad Jon is enjoying himself."

"Thank you, Brian. It's been a good day." Susan looks back down the trail. "I guess I'd better catch up to my guys."

I pour part of the bucket of water on the fire which gives a loud hiss, and a gray cloud filled with ash mushrooms into the trees. A bit more stirring, a bit more water, and the blaze reduces to a warm slush. I recall all my shared campfires and the camaraderie, encircling everyone like the rocks in the fire ring. Raucous laughter, followed by deadened silence, and moments of introspection only a fire can release. And the primordial feeling of warm in front, cold on the back along with the mesmerizing stare into the flames, turning time into an abstraction. A person chucks another piece of wood on the fire and sparks shoot into the night like fireflies dancing. I stare into the tree tops hoping Jon experiences the same connection, and pick up the empty bucket before making my way down the trail.

My kids are back from Parents Weekend and inside the cabin regaling themselves with tales of overeating and golf scores. I sit on the porch in a graying Adirondack chair staring over the lake in the fading purplish light. The fifty-dollar bill rests on the arm of the chair as I wait for the soulful dirge of taps.

A car crunches down the hill on the gravel toward my cabin and parks. I don't recognize the car or the people in it at first. Susan steps out while the others remain in the car.

I meet her at the cabin steps.

"Can we talk for a minute?" Susan says.

Oh, oh. Now what? Susan strikes me as a person not to be quibbled with.

"When I left Jon at his cabin a few parents milled about like usual after drop-offs. I overheard about this bet and realized who was involved."

Where is this going? Maybe she believes her son is a pawn in the bet.

"I asked Jon about Marlon or Dan or whatever his name is. He said Marlon's kind of a jerk. A lot of the kids think that." She looks back at the car as if seeking Jon's assent. "Jon has had his fair share of bullying. This Marlon sounds like a bully and I'm really tired of people like that. So, let's fix things, okay?"

My heart stops racing. "I'd like to, but I owe him fifty bucks."

She holds a 100-dollar bill. "Will that do it?"

The hundred is so crisp it looks newly minted and I'm afraid I'll get a paper cut if I touch it. I find myself reaching for it. I do quick math in my head: 135 dollars from my cabin kids, fifty, plus 100 from Susan. That comes to 285 dollars. So, Marlon's 380 dollars hasn't doubled me after all. It seems wrong to take the money; more than anything though, I want to see Marlon's smug smile fade. "More than do it," I say.

"Good. This has been a wonderful weekend."

We part and she hurries back to the car. I stare at the bill, holding it by the corner between my index finger and thumb as if it shouldn't be soiled by my hand. A chorus of frogs peep from the lake shore and a gentle breeze carries the scent of pine across the water. After a minute, I fold it and it makes a noise like an autumn leaf underfoot before I set it in my shirt pocket and head to the dining hall.

THE DISTANCE BETWEEN
TWO POINTS

I always wondered where the expression "as the crow flies" originated. A crow does a lot of things during a day: scrabbling for a piece of roadkill, fending off territorial interlopers, terrorizing the neighbor's cat, and so on. It doesn't go from A to B in a straight line; it flies from A to B via C, D, M, and Z, which is pretty much the way my life went; it took a lot of extra miles to get where I was going, especially with Mary.

Point A started at a remote Forest Service timber camp in Rodman Bay, thirty air miles north of Sitka, Alaska, in 1978. I clambered off the aluminum ladder-struts of the Beaver into a downpour and waded ashore, met by a stranger clad in Helly Hansen raingear.

A woman's voice said, "Hand me one of those bags." Shouldering my heavy backpack, I passed her my daypack and the box with food, mail, and newspapers.

We stumbled up the cobble-strewn beach, never looking at anything but our feet, all powers of concentration focused on walking on bowling balls while carrying heavy bags. Our hunched-back, face-down approach kept the rain from blowing into our faces.

The alder thicket at tide line gave way to a towering stand of spruce. Four tent platforms lay scattered in a small clearing, and inside was a sodden haven from the wind. We made our way to the farthest one. Inside, I was hit by a blast of warmth emanating from a small oil stove. The stranger I'd followed dropped her hood.

"I'm Mary," she said with a disarming, warm smile. A stream of water trickled down her forehead and dripped off her nose. She extended her hand to me. I shook it, noticing the dirt under her nails.

"You're the new timber cruiser, right?" Mary dropped my wet pack on the floor, wandered over to a coffee pot on the stove and snapped the burner off. "Not much left but you're welcome to it."

"Thanks. I'm Mark, on loan to you guys for the next ten days until something more permanent can be worked out." I slipped the pack off my shoulder, thankful—I'd had the foresight to secure my gear in trash bags before packing it. The box Mary carried from the beach, also swaddled in a plastic bag, got deposited on a table surrounded by eight folding lawn chairs. From past experience, I knew the camp's crew was more anxious for mail than seeing me, so I undid the knotted bag, revealing the box.

Mary pulled a folding Buck knife from her pocket and slit the strapping tape on the box. Paying no attention to the gallon Ziploc bag of Hershey bars on top, she dug until she found a brown padded envelope. "Mail!"

"Newspapers are on the bottom."

Acting as if she didn't hear me, Mary sorted the mail faster than a postal worker before clocking out. She bit her lip upon seeing one address, turned toward me, and said, "What's your name again?"

"Mark."

"Mark, your cot is in the tent on the far left." She picked up her letters and shoved them behind the bib of her Helly pants. "I'm gonna try to find some dry clothes. The rest of the crew is still in the woods. See you at dinner."

I wandered over to my tent and shook off my wet raingear. Three of the four bunks were already claimed, and clothes hung from nails on the two-by-four frame. After unpacking and shoving my gear under the unclaimed bunk, I killed time scanning aerial photos of Rodman Bay's timber until dinner.

Six smelly, dirty crew who looked like they stepped out of a cave painting joined Mary and me for dinner. Between finding dry clothes and chow time, she prepared a mountain of burritos the crew devoured with little conversation other than "pass the Tabasco." It was like a pack of wolves descending on an elk carcass, only slightly less graceful. After third helpings were devoured and the burping stopped, conversation resumed. During dinner, I checked Mary out from the corner of my eye. Her effervescence and self-assured casualness carried over to the after-dinner banter. I listened to the war stories and her repartee with the crew with much interest.

Two days later, Mary took off to visit a sick aunt in Burbank.

Three weeks had passed since Mary's Burbank departure. I was in the Sitka Forest Service bunkhouse, carrying a load of underwear, socks, and shirts along with a pile of sheets from the laundry room to the kitchen table. I'd just started folding them when Mary walked in.

We looked at one another, startled, like two bears suddenly meeting in the woods. She said, "I know you! What's your name again?"

Nice to know my presence at the Rodman Bay camp made such an impact. I finished coupling a pair of socks and set them aside in a pile next to the folded shirts. "Mark—Mark from Rodman Bay. It's okay. It was only for a few days."

She dropped her jacket on the floor, sat down in a kitchen chair, and tugged off her boots. "I never forget a face. Names, on the other hand, I'm not so hot with."

Mary's Pendleton wool shirt didn't smell of sweat or smoke, so I figured she must be on her days off. For the first time, I got the opportunity to really see what she looked like. Stout but not husky, dirty blonde hair, jeans snug around her muscular legs, with a shirt that filled out nicely. I wondered what she saw when she looked at me. My old girlfriend used the term 'easy on the eyes.' I hoped Mary saw me the same way.

"I'm looking for a girl named Sue—I heard she was staying here. Tall. Thin. Pretty. You'd remember her if you saw her," Mary said. She pulled out another chair and set her feet on it. "I'm not sure if I should wait for her or hoof it back downtown."

"Doesn't ring a bell."

"I'll wait a bit and see if she wanders in." Mary eyed my pile of laundry. "You sure do a nice job folding. I can never get them like you do, so I just roll 'em into a ball."

"Not sure if it's a God-given talent or a lot of practice." I eyed the crisp edges on the sheets and shirts and the underwear folded in half and started setting them in the laundry basket.

"I'm gonna give Sue five more minutes and then head out." She pulled the Buck knife out of her back pocket and started cleaning her nails with the blade. "Where'd you say you're from again?"

"Oregon, down on the coast. Little town called Florence. Ever heard of it?" I shoved the laundry aside, following Mary with my eyes as she moved to a weathered sofa set among two armchairs, one with an arm hanging askew. She splayed across the sofa, one leg on it and the other on the floor.

"Passed through there once when I was younger on a trip to Seattle. Don't remember it, though."

"Not surprised. It's pretty small."

Mary peered at her watch. "Time's up. I'm gonna take off. If you see Sue, tell her a bunch of us are meeting at the airport bar at 9:00 p.m." She slid her boots on and plucked her jacket off the floor. "There's a new band in town, and we're going dancing." She paused and faced me. "Stop by the airport if you want, Mark from Rodman Bay."

The bass vibrated so loudly I thought cracks were going to open in the floor before I walked into the bar. The syncopated thud of the drums and flashing lights illuminated a cloud of cigarette smoke hovering over a crowd sitting at the skirt of a small dance floor. I stood near the entrance looking for Mary or anything looking like a group of Forest Service seasonals. A waitress in a tight top scurried by with several drinks on a tray. Unsure if I should return to reading my James Michener book in my bunk, I waded in deeper. As I shouldered past a guy with a logging shirt and suspenders, a sharp yank on my arm turned me around.

"Hey, you made it." Mary smiled. A UCLA tee clung to her and beads of sweat dotted her forehead. "We're over here." She half-danced while pulling me toward a round table on the far side of the floor. "Everyone, this is… Mark. Ha! You thought I forgot your name again, didn't you?"

She laughed, and I wondered how many drinks she'd had. I recognized some people, knew two others, and found myself seated next to a tall, blonde girl.

"Hi, I'm Sue." She extended her hand. "So how do you know Mary?"

"I was out at Rodman Bay with her for two days and ran into her at the bunkhouse today. That's about it. More random than anything."

"Random." She laughed. "That's Mary all right."

The lull between songs ended, and Jackson Browne's "Running on Empty" poured out of the speakers. People flooded the dance floor while I sat rooted to my chair. Mary looked over at me, gesturing with her finger to come join her. I shouted, "I'll sit this one out!" I needed at least one beer before dancing.

Mary shot out of her chair, strode over, grabbed my hand, and pulled me out onto the floor. "This song's too good to sit out."

I didn't return to my seat, as we danced to an odd medley of The Eagles, Fleetwood Mac, Van Halen, and Queen.

"You know, you're not a bad dancer," she said as we leaned on each other while the band was on break, both of us soaked with sweat.

"Thanks for the compliment. Who's my competition?"

"That guy with the suspenders and Mike and Bill from our table. Stone feet—all of them."

The crowd trickled out after another set, and Mary and I caught a cab back to the bunkhouse. In the backseat, her head rested on my shoulder, as she snoozed until the taxi hit a pothole in the bunkhouse parking lot and jarred her awake. "Are we here?"

We stood in the parking lot, unsure of what was going to happen next. "You could come in if you want."

Mary turned, looking down Halibut Point Road. "I'd like to, but I should probably walk to clear my head. I'm crashing at a friend's place." She reached over and gave me a quick kiss on the cheek. A fine mist floated down from the sky. "This was fun. Thanks."

"What are you doing tomorrow?"

"No plans."

"Maybe I'll call."

"Maybe I'll answer."

She cut across the bunkhouse lot and walked the road shoulder toward the ferry terminal. I saw her grow smaller with each receding streetlight she passed under and turned in for the night.

All I had was her number written on the bar napkin I shoved in my pocket the night before. I called. She didn't answer. I gave her the benefit of the doubt, thinking she wasn't home or busy with errands, but wondered if this was the end of the road.

After my days off in Sitka, I was back in the field at another camp. I eavesdropped on radio conversations to see if Mary called with a food order or a flight request from dispatch just to listen to her voice or know where she was. I knew Forest Service seasonals worked in various camps, moving around Southeast Alaska like displaced persons.

The thin line connecting us was withering. I wondered if there ever were any lines. I told myself it was only one night. Was I making too much of it? I sensed this connection I couldn't shake. A karmic force tugging at me as if I had no free will.

With field season over, I headed back to my parents' house in Florence, Oregon, for Thanksgiving, and to sort my options while my room and board were free. On the way to the Sitka airport, I stopped to pick up my mail: paycheck, letter from Mom, letter from my sister, bill, bill, L.L. Bean catalog, postcard. I flipped the card over, wondering who sent me a picture of Crater Lake.

Hey, I'm in Roseburg, Oregon. C'mon down and we can go dancing again. I've got a place you can stay. Hope you can make it! Next to the name "Mary" was a smiley face and a phone number in bold block letters.

No explanation of how she'd disappeared or where she went. *Here I am! Come get me!* Like a stick I was supposed to fetch whenever it was tossed.

In my head, I knew Roseburg and Florence weren't that far apart. At least they were on the same side of the state. I didn't have a firm schedule once I got off the jet in Seattle, so what the hell. A few Greyhound bus legs, and I'd be in Roseburg. I wondered if I was just some dumb golden retriever, running in circles, looking for a stick to chase.

The Roseburg Greyhound terminal phone booth next to the men's room smelled of Pine Sol and urine. The phone book was ripped from its mooring, and several names and numbers were scribbled on the wall. I pulled the card from my shirt pocket, plugged a coin in the slot, and listened to the loud, clicking dial tone.

"Hello?"

"Mary, it's me. Mark. I'm at the bus terminal."

"Woohoo! You came! I wasn't sure you would."

I almost didn't come. I liked to plan. But with Mary, I was moving over new terrain without a map, compass, or my common sense. She was like a chunk of iron totally messing up the magnetic arrow inside me, which always pointed true north. "Here I am. So, where are you?"

"I'll come get you." A *click* indicated she'd hung up.

I slung my backpack over a shoulder, picked up my duffle bag, and shuffled to a wooden bench in front of the terminal, staring at a gray fall sky undecided if it would unleash snow, sleet, or rain. Thankful for the terminal's overhang, I set my pack and duffle on the bench beside me, partly to keep it off the dirty, stained sidewalk, and partly to keep the odd human strays I'd seen in the terminal from sitting next to me. Others had lingered here— the bench was carved with graffiti and highly detailed anatomical drawings.

An orange VW Bug backfired and stopped in front of me. The parking brake crunched, and Mary opened the door, ran over, and hugged me. I wrapped my arms around her, inhaling the sharp zest of Doctor Bronner's Peppermint Soap, the inexpensive and potent favorite in field camps. We stood apart, momentarily admiring each other. Her red down jacket had duct tape on one elbow, and her hair hung down to her shoulders. She hugged me again, this time longer and silently as if we were that Buck knife folding into itself.

"Let's get away from this shithole," she said.

We headed north on Route 99 past a stream of fast-food joints, auto parts stores, and more churches than there are religions, before shifting east. The whole time, Mary filled me in on her life since I'd seen her. I listened but focused on Mary. I saw the gentle curve of her jaw, the cute eye-squinting, the scrunched-up nose. The way her breasts shifted as she went from third to fourth gear like an Indy race car driver.

"We're almost there."

"So where are we headed?"

"I'm crashing at a friend's place. She went to Medford for a week, so we have the place to ourselves." She looked over at me to see how that registered.

I let the comment float by me, untouched.

We pulled into a trailer park and stopped in a muddy cul-de-sac. "Here we are." She grabbed my duffle bag and, though it weighed north of forty pounds, hefted it on to her shoulder with ease.

I flopped on the sofa using my backpack for a footrest, looking forward to settling in, even if it was only for a few days.

Mary sat down beside me, draped a hand on my knee, and laid her head on my shoulder. "I'm really glad you're here."

I put my arm around her and tilted my head toward hers. "I'm glad I came." We sat there for a minute, my mind wondering where I was going, adrift in a raft on a still lake.

Mary stood up and tugged my hand. "C'mon."

The munchies got us out of bed at 11:00 p.m. Mary, shirt-less with my gym shorts on, and me, towel wrapped around my waist. Her butter knife scraped the bottom of the peanut butter jar just as I finished off the saltine crackers. The symmetry struck us, and we burst out laughing, hugging, and toppling onto the mattress on the bedroom floor, before falling asleep, sated in all ways.

It went on for five days: scavenging odd meals at odder hours, exhausting ourselves in bed like spawned-out salmon, dancing at the Lariat until our limbs were limp. A haze settled over us like the damp fog that rolled into Roseburg from the hills. Morning bled into afternoon, which turned to dusk, then dark, as if we were in our own personal time zone.

It was time to go. I promised my parents I would be home for Thanksgiving, now three days away. We sat in the VW at the bus terminal, windshield wipers swishing at the light rain, while we silently contemplated all the roads ahead of us. Two unemployed itinerant Forest Service seasonals with only the homes we grew up in as our true base. Places we'd outgrown but could not leave for good. We lingered at the bus door as long as possible until the bus driver said, "Hey Buddy, kiss her and let's get a move on." I stepped up, and the door hissed shut.

Mary said she'd write or call, although she told me she didn't like talking on the phone much. Either way, not a word from her. It was mid-December, and I was stuck in neutral waiting for the mailman and hoping each ring of the phone might be her. Should I call or wait? It was an age-old dating game I usually lost. I called the Roseburg number.

"Nah, she's not here." Mary's roommate said. "Left about a week ago, kinda on short notice. Sold her car and a few things and said she was heading south." The voice paused as papers rustled in the background. "I think she said California. I have contact info here somewhere. I'll call you when I find it. Okay to call collect?"

"Sure, collect is fine." I carefully recited my phone number twice and hung up. When I didn't hear anything for three days, I tried again. Five times to be exact. In the back of my mind, the road to Mary turned into a dead end.

I hung the dog leash on a peg by the door and handed Dudley, our family lab, a Milk-Bone. The chill from our beach walk started to wear off when my mom said, "You got mail. Who is this Mary, anyway?" She pointed to a wooden side table where the mail was piled. "You never said anything about a Mary."

"You read my mail?"

"I couldn't help but read it. It's a postcard. By the way, when are you going to help take the Christmas lights down?"

One corner of the card was torn, and the other looked like a small rodent nibbled it. The front said, "Greetings from Acapulco." On the back was Mary's looping scrawl: *I got a great place on the beach. Really cheap. Learning to surf (kind of). Come join me. Mary.* There was an address and a strange-looking phone number for a nearby restaurant named Juanita's that could reach Mary. I checked the postmark: December 12th.

I pulled a weathered Rand McNally atlas from our bookshelf and turned to Mexico, straining to find Acapulco. With one finger marking the page, I flipped to California, Oregon, and Mexico to get a sense of how far it was from Florence.

Monarch butterflies migrate from Canada to the mountains of Mexico, and arctic terns flap from the top of North America to Tierra del Fuego. What they follow, nobody really knows. Are there landmarks? Magnetic fields? Celestial navigation? Do they go in a straight line or make side trips to feed or rest? I had no idea where the crows go. All I know is I found my way 2,500 miles to Mexico, Spanish-American paperback dictionary in hand, blinking in the hot sun waiting for Mary to meet me at the Acapulco airport.

A collectivo pulled up to the curb, an overflowing heap of luggage bungee-corded to the top of it. The door swung open, and Mary, tanned and wearing a bikini top and cutoff jeans, spilled out from a wall of bodies packed into the van.

She gave me a big hug, and I felt the warmth of her arms circle me. "Get in. We're headed for Marquelia, about ninety miles south."

She sensed my hesitation as I looked at the tangle of arms, legs, and torsos sandwiched in the van.

"Don't worry. There's room." Her hand was on my back, and I felt it pushing me. Somehow, I made it in, my backpack draped across two strangers' laps. Mary plopped in mine, her arm curling around my neck. "See, I told you there was room." She had a triumphant look on her face as the collectivo belched smoke and pulled away from the curb.

We cut off onto a dirt road for ten miles, a cloud of dust trailing us. The ocean was so close breakers curled in, casting foam on the broad expanse of sand. A town appeared among the swaying palms: shacks with tin roofs, empanada stands, and dilapidated buildings with signs showing, *ferreteria*, where sweaty, shirtless guys with cutting torches disassembled cars. Mangy dogs wandered the streets. Chickens pecked in side yards.

What had I gotten myself into? I just wanted to see Mary, enjoy some sun, and drink cheap margaritas. We could have done that in San Diego or Honolulu, where I could at least order drinks in English.

Mary squeezed my inner thigh, "Don't worry. This will be fun."

The van eased past several pedestrians before turning into a dirt lot next to a convenience store with freshly killed chickens hanging in the window. A guy in a sleeveless tee managed to pry open the door, and a half-dozen of us sprang for the fresh air.

Backpack on, Mary grabbed my hand and said, "This way." Two dogs followed us, and Mary pulled some dog treats from her pocket. "Here, Paco." The dog munched the treat. "I don't know this other guy, but he's kinda cute." Half his ear was gone, an abscess wept on his side, and his tail was missing a chunk of fur. Mary tossed his treat on the ground, and we kept moving.

We passed through two side streets with signs for hostels and cheap rooms when Mary said, "Here we are." Three rough-hewn, graying wood cabanas with tin roofs nestled under a grove of palms at the edge of the beach. "We're in the one on the right." She pulled a small key from her shorts, and the front door creaked open. Inside, two single beds were pushed together. The propane fridge and small two-burner stove sat wedged next to open cupboards with plates, cups and bowls, and a tiny sink drained into a five-gallon bucket. A jug of drinking water was perched on the other side of the counter. "The bathroom and more drinking water are at Juanita's restaurant down that alley. She rents the place."

Juanita was a heavyset, formidable entrepreneur with a family empire engulfing the town of Marquelia. She owned two restaurants, one hotel, and the cabanas. Need a bike tire fixed? See her cousin, Heraldo. The freshest chickens? Try her brother, Manuel. Plumbing problems? Her uncle, Jorge, could fix anything.

Mary let the cabana's cheap slat blinds down on three sides and set the ocean-side blinds at half-mast so the breeze could waft in. She had already removed her top and was stepping out of her shorts.

The next week, we lazed around, wandered to the local market mangling the little Spanish I gleaned from my dictionary, and sampled every bar and empanada stand in town. I took surfing lessons from Juanita's brother, Felipe, who provided the bulk of his guidance from the beach, sitting in a *palapa's* shade, knocking back cervezas.

Despite generous applications of Coppertone, my white skin turned shades of red I never knew existed. Mary tended me lovingly, but body contact was painful, the merest touch scorching like a scorpion sting. For two days, I lay in bed, praying for the cool ocean breeze to filter in and wrap me in its embrace. I stared at the corrugated aluminum roof until I saw images and shapes in the folds of metal.

Emerging like a mole from underground, I stepped from the cabana in a tee and broad-brimmed straw hat. One day we rented bikes from Heraldo and peddled to a nearby beach where a man approached us while we lolled on our blanket and offered two ice creams for free. He worked at a small *palapa* down the beach and thought we might be hot. Two days later, Juanita left fresh tamales for us. The sense of community of our beach town, with the laughter and strong family ties, made me wonder why these people, so obviously poor, seemed to enjoy life more than people in Roseburg or Florence.

In the evening, we'd find a small, quiet restaurant with just locals and enjoy the friendly banter, even if it only consisted of a few words or gestures. The cool of night brought out singing, guitars, mescal, and tequila.

It only took nine days for me to exhaust pretty much everything there was to do in and around Marquelia. That included getting sunburned and recovering for two days. I hadn't learned the fine art of doing nothing and knowing it is okay. Mary had mastered it and found more ways to do nothing than anyone I ever knew.

On more than one occasion, Mary got up from our table and sauntered over to laugh with some of the Mexicans while I sat in my plastic lawn chair under a string of colored electric lights, nursing my margarita. The men laughed, and words like "*mujer caliente*" and "*hermosa mujer*" drifted to me in the night air. Twice, a mariachi band played, and Mary was asked to dance. The Mexicans looked at me, and I was unable to decipher their thoughts. The foreign music and different culture left me unsure of myself. Was I failing to amuse her, or was I jealous of their attention? Or both? I couldn't help but wonder if I was a redundant part of this vacation.

The surf roared in the background as we lay on our backs underneath a threadbare sheet in our tiny cabana. Only minutes before, we grunted in unison, our bodies enmeshed like two breeding anacondas, only pausing when

Mary accidently knocked over the small night table lamp. The gasping ceased, and a stillness settled. Mary ran her hand across my chest, making small, twirly circles.

Her hand stopped moving. "We're not really much alike."

I turned toward her, staring into eyes as blue as the lagoon down the coast. Her mouth, normally a cat-like smile, was a thin, flat line. "When did you realize that?"

"I kinda knew it all along but never needed to say it."

"You *needed* to say it?"

"I guess it was time," Mary sat up, holding the sheet against her breasts like armor. "We're not really compatible. I mean we get along and all that, but—"

"But what?" I was more than hurt. I was cut deeply—though I realized she was right. I hadn't wanted to admit it and didn't want too now.

"You don't really relax." Mary pulled more of the sheet around her, uncovering me. "Kind of like you're on guard all the time. I don't get it."

Mary's window into my personality unsettled me. I recognized she was more perceptive than I was, which rattled me more. Her flair for life, scattered manner, and derring-do in bed blinded me to what our relationship was about and where it was going. My natural reaction was normally to deploy a defensive shield to block her words, although I knew Mary could easily knock it aside.

"Am I right? Are you going to say something?" Mary got out of bed, the sheet half-wrapped around her, part toga, part sarong. She opened the blinds a bit more and seemed to stare far out to sea.

I let out a sigh. "I guess you're right. I don't have your ability to go with the flow." It felt like we were out on the dance floor, dancing by ourselves at opposite ends until the music stopped. "Was this whole thing just about sex?" I spat it at her, knowing it would sting. It wasn't that way for me. But what was it? I wanted more, but maybe I desired it so badly because I knew I couldn't have it. I fell through a trap door and hit bottom.

"No. Well, yes. Kind of. It was more than that, and you damn well know it." Mary opened the small fridge and took out a beer. Instead of opening it, she placed it on her forehead, moving it slowly side to side. "We had fun. We laughed and were silly. We talked about life. And yes, the sex was sensational. I'm not apologizing for anything, and I don't expect you to either."

I sat naked at the edge of the bed. "So, what do we do now?"

We had less and less to say to each other over the next two days before I could get a flight back to the States. A tropic torpor set in. The silence weighed down everything and gnawed, like the worms that left tunnels in the beach logs we'd seen on our walks. Mary disappeared for long beach walks. I read in the lumpy bed and ate my rice and beans alone at Juanita's.

Mary insisted on accompanying me on the clammy collectivo ride back to the airport. We sat side by side like statues, not making eye contact. As the driver unloaded the collectivo at the terminal entrance, Mary turned toward me, tears glistening in her eyes. We were way stations before the next person in our lives showed up. A long journey in a short time without knowing which way we were going. Now we knew. I couldn't change who I was any more than birds can change their migration routes. We were two crows flying in different directions. The hot buzz of hormones and infatuation flared until the final lick of flame guttered out.

No theatrics, no fireworks at the end—we weren't those kinds of people. A parting of minds before the stakes got higher. We couldn't check all our emotions at the door. She put her arms around me, tears wetting my shirt. I held her tight and laid my head in the crook at the base of her neck, not wanting to move.

"*Vámanos!*" The driver tapped his horn gently.

I kissed her gently on the cheek, tasting the salty smoothness. "Drop me a card."

"Okay, I will." She pulled a red bandana from a back pocket and blotted tears.

I knew this was the last I'd hear from her.

The driver honked more insistently.

"Time for me to go." Anything I wanted to say was a cliché, a goodbye from a Bogart movie. I put my pack on and headed for the automatic glass doors of the terminal. I passed below a light stanchion with a crow perched on it. Before reaching the door, I turned to see Mary. The crow *caw-cawed*, and the collectivo was gone.

Inside, I set my daypack on a molded plastic seat and checked to make sure I had my return ticket, finding it exactly where I'd left it. As I set the ticket back, my fingers felt the tiny Spanish-American dictionary nestled in my palm. With my thumb, I riffed the pages once and set it down on the seat. Perhaps a new traveler could use it.

* * *

You can be a butterfly, an arctic tern, or a crow, but the path in life is not between two points. It is more like a circle, maybe one that doesn't close. And all roads don't have to lead somewhere.

INTO THE BLACK

Dana signed on with the Lolo Hotshots as the only female on the crew. One guy was a perv, two believed farting was hysterical, a handful were hardened misogynists, and the rest treated you the way you wanted to be treated. All had your back if you needed it. And then, there was Troy.

Troy was the person in the center of every crew picture, even if he had to wedge in. His hurricane-force persona combined with raven-black hair and country-boy smile made more than one guy say, "Watch out for Troy. He's a real player."

Just, what I need, Dana groused.

Dana and Troy didn't spend much time working together since they were in different squads. He was a rooster, though, and she was the sole hen on the crew so Dana's antennae were always up.

The crew paused on a ridge, and Troy lay next to her and rearranged an item in his line gear and used it as a pillow. His Pulaski, a combination ax and hoe, lay next to him. Dana sucked from a long tube attached to a water bladder in her pack. It was 3:00 p.m. and her throat was parched and raw from the smoke-filled air. She lay sprawled in the dirt with her leather gloves on her chest and her head propped on a log. They were frazzled trying to beat the beast back. With the climate changing, the fires burned hotter, and each day's perils made them wonder how much longer they could protect the sheds, barns, and McMansions encroaching on the headwaters of each valley.

"When was the first time you went into the black?" Troy asked. He was referring to the burned-over portion of a fire; it could be charred lodgepole pine, wheatgrass, shrubby manzanita, or whatever. The blackened ground was their safety zone—a place they could escape as a last resort. A site that wouldn't feed the oncoming flames.

She was surprised Troy asked a question. He hadn't shown much interest in her beyond basic fire line exchanges. "I'm not sure," Dana said. "I think it was on the Gemini Fire." She fingered her necklace.

"Why are you always fiddling with that thing?" Troy asked.

She had not realized she was touching the necklace. "I don't know." Tucking it under her fraying cotton shirt, she offered, "A habit I picked up." She didn't want to go into too much detail: how she found the cheap necklace at a garage sale, how the "S" in the circle didn't stand for a middle name, a boyfriend's name, or anything like that. To her, it meant "survivor" and it was a talisman, crazy in a way, to help keep the demons at bay.

"Kind of like a lucky charm, right?" Troy said.

"I guess so."

Their crew boss walked up to them, a cloud of dust trailing him. "We're pulling out," the boss said. "The fire's getting unpredictable and the forecast is for steadily increasing wind."

Dana looked at the half-mile of line they had just carved out for seven hours. They were abandoning it. It was the right call.

"We'll regroup and tackle it again tomorrow from a safer place," the crew boss said.

The next morning before they got in the rigs, the crew boss called Troy and Dana over. "Troy, I'd like you to be lookout for the crew today. Take Dana with you and show her the ropes." A burst of chatter blared on his radio and he turned the volume down. "We gotta build her cred in camp."

Dana wondered how awkward it might get after several hours staring at a fire with Troy. Thankful for the opportunity to gain new experience, Dana shrugged. *How bad could it be?*

Dana and Troy huffed their way through the woods, crossed a steep ravine, and traveled up a ridge. Now three-quarters of a mile from the crew, they had a good view of the terrain and the fire down the valley in front of them. Their crew depended on the two of them keeping an eye on the flames.

"I know one thing," Troy said. "We're not going back the way we came if there's a problem. We'd never make it out of that ravine."

Dana stared down at the couloir and its tangle of downed timber, boulders, and thick brush. "No shit."

Troy scanned the area on the other side of the ridge from the fire's direction. "There's a small meadow down there. It's not as big as I'd like it to be, but it's our best option for our safety zone." He handed her the binos. "What do you think?"

"I wish it was a few hundred yards closer and thirty yards wider."

"Me too," Troy said.

"What's the crew's trigger point?" Dana asked.

"When the fire reaches the bottom of our ravine, the crew's gotta get the hell out. The fire will sweep right up that like a chimney."

Dana was aware of how fast a fire, pushed by wind, could travel up a steep slope. The names of fires where crews perished trying to outrun a wall of flame were seared into the minds of firefighters.

They parked themselves against several large boulders and smaller rocks as the morning heat built. For the next few hours, a carousel of air tankers dropped retardant and helicopters slung buckets of water on the blaze. The fire swatted away those efforts as smoke and flames rolled up from the valley and grew in size and intensity, like a pot ready to boil over. Steady banter flowed over the crew and air-to-ground radio channels, relaying fire behavior, weather data, and crew locations.

Smoke clouds ascended to the jet stream and billowed to the north and west. Dana always imagined faces in the clouds; she saw Uncle Don and his malicious smile as he cornered her in the basement bathroom. She knew the words: Stop. Don't. No. Quick gasps left her suffocated and mute. *This isn't happening. This isn't happening.*

Springing to her feet, she grabbed several egg-sized rocks and threw them down the ravine with such force she grunted, *Unnhh,* after each throw.

"What was that all about?" Troy asked.

In her fury, she had forgotten Troy was there. Like she had blacked out and snapped back to consciousness. Dana dropped the last stone. "Nothing," Dana lied. "I just like throwing rocks."

Troy looked at her. "That was a little weird. I know firefighting is pretty tough, especially for a lone chica, but you're wrapped pretty tight by any standard."

Dana sat down again. "Maybe so."

"Big talker too." Troy sucked down half a water bottle. "How'd you get into this racket?" He asked.

"I guess I needed a mental diversion." Dana had battled with herself ever since her bathroom entrapment, and there were times she wasn't sure she was going to win. It was a titanic effort to keep from collapsing like a star sucked into a black hole. She medicated by dosing with long runs, solo backpacks, and CrossFit. "Exercise helps. What about you?"

"Small town. Single mom. Not many choices and the ones I made didn't always turn out so hot. Mostly juvenile stuff: racing cars, drinking beer, goofing around. Nothing that got me tossed in jail." Troy shuffled his feet, his boot plowing a pile of stones. "With hotshot OT, the money is good and like most of us, a shot of adrenaline doesn't hurt now and then. The other option was the military but I'm not cut out for that."

Dana studied Troy from behind the shield of her reflective sunglasses. Maybe the guys on the crew were busting her balls about Troy.

They ate their boxed lunches while Troy periodically picked up the binoculars to offer play-by-play. "I think the New Mexico crew is working the line on the next ridge." He pointed to a helicopter maneuvering with a bucket. "They're gonna drop water down the hill from them to cool things off."

Dana wanted to shout into the radio, "Go home. None of this is working! It's bigger than us!" After years witnessing burns with increasing fury, she could spot a futile effort. All the he-man, can-do bullshit never ceased. She shook her head. The climate was changing but nothing else was.

Troy watched the fire with growing concern. He'd stop and assess the wind direction and strength. "I don't like the looks of this." A steady breeze rustled the trees near them, and more black smoke roiled from the basin below. Suddenly, a whole side of the valley ignited in a fireball with a thunder carrying to the ridge.

"Jesus!" Dana said.

Troy keyed the radio mic to update the crew. "Guys, this is blowing up. Stay on your toes. You may need to leave in a hurry."

Troy bit his lip as he peered into the binoculars. Dana knew he was gauging the fire's distance to the ravine—the trigger point—where the crew needed to be alerted.

The wind asserted itself again and the fire shot ahead, consuming five acres in the time it took to inhale and exhale. Flames spiraled and embers rained down near them, creating small spot fires. "Pull the plug, guys. It's making a run," Troy yelled into the radio. "Dana, grab your stuff. We need to get out of here too."

Dana had close calls before but this fire had a mind of its own. It grew bigger and faster than any fire she'd ever observed before. *We have an escape route and a safety zone.* It calmed her momentarily but she couldn't shake her premonition: this was different.

They picked up their tools and line gear and Troy scurried off over downed logs, busting through the brush.

She tried to keep up with him, carrying a Pulaski in one hand and thirty-five pounds on her back. Troy stopped and waved his hand. "C'mon!" When she caught up with him, he said, "You lead and I'll follow so we can stick together better. Move your butt." He grinned and shoved her forward. A branch whipped her face, stinging her cheek, without slowing her. She couldn't see the fire but knew from the size of the embers pelting the ground, the smoke building in the woods, and the hellish roar, that it must have crested the ridge.

After scampering a half-mile or more, they stopped at the safety zone, each of them hunched over, catching their breath. The fire, buoyed by a late-afternoon wind, pushed flames through the upper area they had just passed through.

"We need to clear this out," Troy said. "We can't outrun this."

They grubbed down to bare soil, ripping the grass and anything else that could burn and cast it aside.

Dana studied the small meadow. It was tight—the fire might get too close. Her arms pumped as she scraped and chopped, fueled by an overdose of adrenaline. She didn't want to look up again. Fear pulsed through her. *Dig! Dig! Dig!* A bull elk ran into their small clearing, the whites of its eyes flashed, and nostrils flared in the smothering smoke, before it clattered off. Dana wanted to climb on its back—except she couldn't leave Troy. They were in this together, for better or worse.

The wind grew as if the fire spawned its own. Twigs and pine needles flew by. Trees exploded sending flames hundreds of feet in the air. A deafening roar surrounded them.

"Get in your shelter!" Troy yelled.

Dana could barely hear him only ten feet away. "What?"

Troy pointed to the five-pound, aluminum-coated fabric fire shelter they carried on their line gear belts. Once inside, it deflected the worst of the heat. "Get in!" He repeated.

"What about you?" She screamed, her voice carrying into the trees.

"I've got to burn this off," Troy said. He pointed to the grass surrounding their small excavated area. "We need to be in the black."

Dana pulled the water bladder from her pack and dropped it at her feet. She grabbed the fire shelter from its compartment and tossed her gear and Pulaski away so they wouldn't ignite close to the deployed shelter. She had practiced this for years and while part of it was reflex, there was no simulating this terror. The wind whipped the fabric shelter, blowing so hard she had to stand on the bottom of the shelter and pull it over her like a cape. Before she lay down with the shelter draped over, she glanced at Troy, an apparition in the smoke-choked clearing. He had lit a fusee—essentially a road flare—and touched the knee-high grass which burned quick and hot, leaving a protective singed area around them.

Inside the shelter it was less smoky and hot, but enough smoke and heat had entered with her that she coughed and her face glowed. She had her hard hat, gloves, water, and a fire-resistant shroud pulled up all the way over her eyeballs to keep the smoke out. Life had come down to a few possessions. Her eyes and throat burned, and the realization that most firefighters die from heat-damaged lungs and airways, not from burns, terrified her, but all she could think about was Troy. Where was he?

A disembodied voice called and she felt a tug on her shelter. "Let me in," Troy hollered.

Dana was stunned. Troy had his own shelter. What happened to his? The shelters were designed for one person, and two people partnering lessened the odds for both. But there was no way she was going to deny him since it was not survivable outside.

Troy wedged into the shelter, half on top of Dana. "It fucking blew away. I had the shelter out, it was in my hand, and then it was gone."

"Let's seal this along the ground so more smoke doesn't get in," Dana said. They were side-by-side yet still yelling over the fire's thundering. The turbulence kicked up by the blaze threatened to tear the shelter off them. Trees crashed in the wind and detonated in blasts as the fire devoured everything in its path. "Jesus, Troy, are we gonna die?"

Troy looked at her and shoved her head down. "Dig a hole in the dirt with your hands and get your mouth as close to the ground as possible." He dug as well, as the heat built inside their shelter and the wind screamed. Giant embers pelted the shelter, rattling it like hail. "We're gonna make it."

Dana didn't want to die but this was certainly hell. Entombed in a thin, shiny shelter, she focused on slow breathing and trying to stay calm. Troy's weight pressed down on one side, insulating her from that side of the fire. It reminded her of Uncle Don cramming her against the bathroom vanity. Hands searching, grabbing. The stink of his beer breath.

Trees crashed to the ground nearby and it brought her back to poor Troy; he must be roasting worse than she was. She sipped water and passed the mouthpiece to him.

"Thanks, I didn't have time to grab my water." Troy said. "I've got to call and let the boss know we've deployed our shelter and we're okay." Coughing several times, he spoke into the radio, letting them know the time of deployment.

Over a connection crackling with static, they made out, "Thank God. Hang in there."

They settled in to survival mode, listening to flames cauterizing every flammable object. She had signed up to fight fires hoping the backbreaking work and fire line rush would purge Uncle Don from her brain. It wasn't working.

"You know, I'm not a jerk like you might think," Troy said.

"I never said you were a jerk." The inferno surged overhead and Dana imagined they were in an aluminum-lined confessional. Or coffin. She welcomed the conversation—anything from dwelling on the hellscape outside.

"Did you believe it?"

Dana realized Troy wanted to know. "Honestly, I don't know what to think anymore." She reflected on all the fires they'd been on together. He had left her alone—never condescended or harassed, which was all she asked of anyone. Firefighting allowed her to shunt memories and focus on primal thoughts: watch your step and don't get burned alive. Look where that had gotten her.

"I like to enjoy life. It's way too short to dwell on the bad shit," Troy said.

"Maybe you could give me a few lessons on that," said Dana as she shifted her body so her arm wasn't numb.

Troy's head mashed against hers. There was no space to move away. He smelled of smoke, sweat, and dirt. Dana's breaths came in small ragged inhalations as her head grew woozy. Her lightheadedness passed. It pissed her

KEN POST · 151

off that Uncle Don stole her ability to enjoy intimacy, and it angered her even more that she continued to let it piss her off.

"Are you okay?" Troy asked. "We got this, right?" His arm draped over her, a gloved hand by her waist. He turned his head to look at her directly. "Right?"

Troy's blackened face glistened and she stared into his smoke-reddened eyes. Flecks of dirt and ash dotted his face.

Troy must have known she was frayed. "Think of your family and friends," Troy said. "They'll want to see you again. I know mine will."

Dana knew the game; everyone had talked during shelter deployment training about staying positive, and she appreciated Troy for helping her focus. It helped when you're stuck in a seven-foot silver cocoon with flames whirlpooling around you.

The shelter almost pulled from their grip as the whirlwind increased. Smoke and hot air in came in through several small tears where the shelter had been folded. An eerie orange glow swept back and forth through the slits. It took all of Dana's effort to keep from snapping; the heat and smoke, the unnerving crescendo, and the helplessness threatened her sanity. She lost all sense of time—how long had they been inside?

She sensed Troy was also struggling. In his position, he took a lot of heat and grew quieter while his breathing became more labored. With her face pushed in the dirt, she squeezed his forearm with her gloved hand. He signaled back by squeezing hers.

Her body had tensed for so long trying to hold the shelter down, an ache burned in Dana's arms and legs.

The wind and heat had died down. "Take a look outside, Troy. Can we leave?"

Troy peered out the bottom of the shelter and smoke and heat slipped in. "Not yet, but it's better. The flame front has passed."

"How long have we been here?" Dana asked.

"I'm not sure. But I'll check." Troy wasn't wearing his watch; it had gotten too hot on his wrist. He pulled it from the dirt. "Forty-five minutes," Troy said.

"More like forty-five fucking hours," Dana said.

Fifteen minutes later, they crawled out of their shelter, coughing and wheezing in the smoke. "Holy shit," Dana said. All around were blackened trees, tendrils of flame curling from them. The sun was barely visible in the gloom and Dana sank to her knees and wept, thrilled to be alive, thankful Troy had been with her. She wasn't sure if she could have survived without him—the solace of another human in a fire-breathing, lifeless world.

Troy kneeled and hugged her. "I was scared shitless," Troy said. "Don't tell anybody." He smiled and wiped her tears with a ragged handkerchief.

They stayed like that, smoke wafting past. It had been a long time since she leaned into a man's hug and welcomed it, letting it flow through her. Tears washed a path through the soot and dirt on Dana's face, and black snot flowed from her nose. She hated to show weakness to Troy or anyone else on her crew. She had fought so hard to keep it together and none of that mattered now.

Troy pulled off his Nomex neck shroud and Dana saw a layer of skin attached to it. "Oww! Fuck!" Troy yelped.

The back of Troy's neck was a blistered mess from the radiant heat that had passed through the shelter. He dropped the shroud on the ground.

"Jesus, Troy. We need to get those burns treated. Don't even think about taking your shirt off until you're back in town." She marveled at Troy's stoicism. He had borne the brunt of the heat with his body so close to the protective lining.

"We need to let the crew know we're alive," Troy said. He helped Dana to her feet. Troy announced over the radio, "We're out, we made it."

"Fantastic!" the crew boss whooped. They heard the boss shout to the others on their crew, "They're out!" Followed by a loud cheer. "Can a chopper land where you're at?"

Troy looked around at the scorched surroundings, engulfed in a netherworld between day and night. "I think so, once the smoke clears," he said.

Dana staggered around their clearing in disbelief. Her mind raced back to the heart of the fire's attack and she doubted she could handle the psychological torment again. She nudged the remnants of her smoldering pack with her foot. In many ways, that pack was part of her. She bent down and picked up one of the few items left unburned: a Swiss army knife, a gift from the crew after her first season as a hotshot. Dana picked it up with her gloved hand and let it cool before putting it in her shirt pocket. She was taking so little, and leaving so much behind.

"Don't go anywhere. You need to be checked out by a medical team," the crew boss said.

She was done. Flat-out done. Done with Uncle Don's skeletons. Done with fires blow-torched by banshee winds that made them sprint up mountains, and consume valleys in seconds. And push firefighters to the brink. She couldn't deal with this anymore on her own.

Dana yanked the chain from her neck and flung it deep into the black. It tumbled in an arc and landed with a small puff of ash.

Troy turned to her and said, "Help is on the way."

WAVES

Josh Putnam laid on his back underneath the cabin, staring at the floorboards and the spiderwebs draped across the joists. He was sandwiched next to a pile of pink rigid foam boards he'd cut to fit as insulation between the joists. Light spilled in from the edges but in the center, it was so dim he switched on a headlamp. It reminded him of hunkering in trenches and sandbag fortifications in Afghanistan. Josh instinctively reached over for Nate, who had been always by his side, only to feel cool gravel and dirt. It did not take much to know how close everyone was to returning to dust and loam.

The cabin seemed to press down, so Josh flipped over and scrabbled on his belly out from below the cabin, resting spread-eagle in the sunlight. His breath came in ragged gulps until he shut his eyes and told himself, *You've got this.* He concentrated on the distinct rise and fall of his chest, and the 'episode,' as his VA counselor had informed him, would pass.

Memorial Day approached and Josh was excited to have his brother Mark, his wife Sarah, and their kids, Dwight and Maddie, visit to show off his progress on the cabin. After months of yelling, sulking, or disappearing into his black funk, they had exiled him in April to the 200 acres of prime Putnam lakeshore their family had owned for over 150 years. Josh's mission was to fix the family cabin that had been neglected since he graduated high school, and get his PTSD under control. The clipboard hanging on a nail by the door with Josh's to-do list had lots of lines crossed out, and Josh felt pretty good, getting something positive done in his life.

Dwight and Maddie sprinted down to the small dock where the skiff was tied up. "Can we go in the boat?" they cried in unison.

"Whoa, whoa!" Sarah shouted. "They've been cooped up in the car and all they've been talking about is going out on the lake with Uncle Josh." She reached into the back of the car and produced two tiny life jackets and handed them to Josh. "Make sure they keep these on."

Crossing the lake, Dwight held the tiller with Josh as the flat-bottomed jon boat pushed across the water. Maddie lay down in front, one hand skimming the lake.

"What's that?" Dwight asked. He pointed to an old rock chimney and foundation. It was near the shore and a house was farther up the slope. The Platé compound.

"It's a fishing lodge that burned a long time ago," Josh said.

Maddie pulled in a length of rope dangling over the gunwale. "Why did it burn up? Were they playing with matches?"

Josh popped the shifter into neutral and the boat idled. "I don't know." Josh didn't tell them the lodge fire set off the 100-year-old Platé-Putnam fight. He didn't mention the Platés accused the Putnams of setting the blaze because the Putnams were pissed off about Platé lodge clients overfishing the lake. And he certainly didn't tell them the Putnam family home, its foundation remnants a sunken pit, mysteriously burned a month after the lodge fire. For as long as he could remember his family had skirmished with the Platé's. Grandpa had told Josh, "They're damned frog-eaters from Quebec. Even the Canadians ran 'em out of their country."

The Putnams even deliberately mispronounced their name: Plate as in dinner plate, knowing the former Québecois hated mispronounced French. They tweaked their current nemesis, Benoit, by calling him Benny to his face.

Josh overhead all the stories as a kid, and they traveled like waves on the lake across generations, washing ashore at the foot of their cabin. He was trying to tamp down his own fires, and he didn't feel obligated to inspire another generation of Platé-hating Putnams for events that happened so long ago.

Two jet skiers roared by as Josh rounded Miller's Point. They were not allowed on the lake, which also had a ten-horsepower limit, but these hotshots never paid attention. Their foaming wake was a close, rolling chop so he yanked the tiller and turned the boat directly into the wave so they didn't take it broadside. "Hold on!" Josh shouted and latched on to Dwight. The boat thumped over the wake and shuddered while Maddie was knocked to the boat floor. "Fuckers!" Josh screamed as the jet skiers zoomed across the lake. "Everybody okay?" he asked.

Maddie landed on a seat cushion and the anchor rope, and was unhurt. She turned to Josh. "That's a bad word, isn't it?"

"Yeah, it is."

"Don't worry, I won't tell," she said.

"Thanks, Maddie." His head pulsed and the tiller hand sweated as he putted back to the cabin at a slow crawl. They hadn't been attacked, although the rapid evasive action sparked memories of his buddies diving for fox-holes, and his Humvee swerving to avoid IEDs and crazed mujahideen.

Josh had made the forty-five-minute drive to the VA and capped off his therapy session with a sundae at Wanda's Ice Cream Parlor. Walking back, he spotted his black Ford pickup and someone sitting on the tailgate he had not left down—Benny—nonchalantly eating an ice cream cone and reading his phone.

"Yo, Benny," Josh said. "What are you doing? You know this is my truck?"

Benny feigned surprise. "Your truck? I didn't know that. I thought you were MIA or AWOL," Benny said. A chipped-tooth smile creased a face with a broad nose and dark eyebrows.

"Cut the shit, Benny. I don't know what your problem is," Josh said.

Benny held his hands out, palms up. "Problem? What problem?"

This passive-aggressive behavior had gone on for years and Josh was weary of it. There were fights, other times, minor vandalism—enough to prick the Putnams. Years ago, his great-grandfather flashed curses in French with the cabin lights using Morse code he'd learned during WWI. The lights blinked across the lake to the Platés' house, igniting another round of mischief.

Benny was the current dilemma. "If you don't get off," Josh said, "I'm gonna drive to the police station, with you hanging off the tailgate. I'll let you sort it out with the cops." Maybe grandpa was right; there wasn't one good apple in a whole barrel of Platés.

"Okay, I'm going. I'm going." Benny gently closed the tailgate. "We're good, right?"

"Yeah, really good, Benny."

Benny smirked, "Hey, thanks for your service."

His tone was not thankful. *His service.* What did that mean anymore? Josh slammed the tailgate shut and drove into the parking lot of an auto parts store. He stared out the windshield and rubbed his temples for a minute.

The occasional pop and crack of pre-Fourth of July firework celebrations the past few days reminded Josh of small arms firing, and though he'd been preparing for it, he was on edge more than he had been in weeks. He bought noise-cancelling headphones and a thick eye mask, took his Prozac, and stepped up his relaxation and visualization exercises. Whatever craziness that happened on the Fourth, it was all in God's hands, except Josh hadn't believed in God for years, and, after Afghanistan, he wasn't confident what he believed in.

Kids had been buzzing around the lake on jet skis all afternoon setting up for a big Fourth of July party on Hatch Island, at the end of the lake. The island's sandy beach and flat campsites attracted Josh's crowd when he was younger. All he did was drink too many Narragansetts, and lose his virginity there, before passing out. These kids took it to the next level, though; stronger drugs, more horsepower, worse attitudes.

The evening darkened and the headlights on the jet skis were all that was visible until a flash of fireworks illuminated the shoreline like a combat flare. A loud boom carried across the lake and echoed off the mountains, and it was time for Josh to put on his headphones and eye mask, and lay down. His playlist had a nice mix of waves, flowing water, wind, and bird sounds to ease his mind.

He didn't know how long he'd been in bed, the cabin had cooled, and a strong breeze carried a hint of ozone. Looking out the window, the lights of the jet skis were visible until the heavens unloaded and sheets of rain blotted his view. His own dock wasn't distinguishable until a bolt of lightning cut through the deluge. He wouldn't want to be out on the lake in this storm.

He went into the bathroom with his headphones on. The warble of birds and a serenade of crickets filtered into his ears. It could have been a Costa Rican rainforest or the depths of the Amazon for all he cared. A persistent banging intruded and Josh removed the headphones. Two soaked teenagers in shorts and t-shirts stood shivering in the cabin entry.

"Mister, we need your help!" the boy yelled.

The girl's lips were blue and she quaked uncontrollably. Josh got out of bed and looked closer. Tears flowed past the water draining from her hair.

"What? Tell me!" The boy was paralyzed so Josh shook him.

"Our friends—on the jet skis—" the boy stammered.

"They got caught in the storm," the girl finished the sentence. "We paddled a canoe here, the nearest place. Can you call for help?"

She shook so violently Josh sat her on the bed so she didn't fall over. "There's no cell service anywhere near here." The boy stared into space, and Josh checked his pupils. "We need to warm you two up." He opened a closet door and pulled out a pile of old army surplus wool blankets. "Use the bathroom to take your wet clothes off and wrap yourself in this blanket." The girl hesitated and looked sideways at the boy. "Do it!" He gestured to the boy. "You're next."

With the kids cocooned in blankets, Josh pulled back the bed covers. "Into bed—both of you," he ordered. "You need to warm up and body heat will help." Tucking the bedspread up to their chins, both looked like they were going to sleep as he spoke. He didn't think to ask their names and mentally assigned them, 'Dick' and 'Jane.' Josh stopped at the cabin door; what had made their jet-skiing friends go out during an approaching thunderstorm? It put everyone's lives in jeopardy.

A thousand other questions zinged in Josh's brain as his army training kicked in; he had to look for the jet skiers. *Nobody gets left behind.*

The truck keys were on a peg by the door. He removed them and stashed the keys in his dirty laundry basket. Josh didn't want the kids pulling any other brainless stunts like grabbing his truck and going for help. In their condition, they wouldn't make it up the quarter-mile driveway without ramming a tree. Inside the porch, Josh pulled on a rain jacket, pants, and a pair of rubber boots, yanked a Red Sox hat low on his head, and cinched a life jacket around himself. *Locked and loaded.* After taking a deep breath, he clicked on the headlamp and dashed to his boat.

The boat lay half-submerged by rain and he wind-mill-bailed with the cutoff milk jug he kept tied to a cleat. He had enough gas in the tank to run all over the lake if he had to—assuming he could see anything. The headlamp beam hardly penetrated the blowing murk and he was flying blind. Waves slapped the boat and threatened to add to the rain already refilling it, so he bailed with his right hand and steered with the left.

An object bumped the boat as he passed by—a riderless jet ski floated on its side. Josh shifted to neutral and scanned the water, listening for a voice. Rain poured down so hard it was like the lake was boiling, and any other sound was drowned out. A stream trailed off the bill of his cap and Josh stared into the white pool of headlamp beam at the bottom of the boat. He decided to make an expanding concentric circle around the jet ski to search for anyone in the water. What else could he do? If only the rain stopped.

The circle pattern didn't produce results. Hoping not to miss anything, he cruised so slowly it was like he was not moving. *There! What's that?* He wanted to find those kids so badly he didn't know if he imagined an object at the far end of the shaft of light. Josh shifted into neutral again and let the boat drift alongside. A person in a blue windbreaker was clinging to a boat cushion.

On his knees in three inches of water sloshing on the floor, Josh leaned over the gunwale and tugged the collar, and the head lolled, facing Josh. It was Benny.

Benny was barely conscious as Josh tried to lift him into the boat but he was too heavy. Josh ran the anchor line under Benny's armpits to keep his head out of the water and lashed the line to a cleat. "Benny, I'm going to have to tow you home. Hang on." Which way was home? The rain had let up a bit although it was pitch-black. Josh pulled a compass from his pocket and watched the red arrow orient to north. He got his bearings, hoping to get close enough to glimpse his cabin's lights.

It was a fine line getting home quickly to keep Benny alive, or slowly to ensure he didn't slide out of the jerry-rigged harness. Benny coughed and sputtered a few times as waves washed over him which was a good sign he was breathing. Josh was back in battle and all he wanted was for everyone to come back in one piece.

Easing the boat ashore at the cabin, Josh jumped out and dragged Benny on to the sandy beach and Benny vomited. Josh's arms slipped through his armpits and he dragged him up the stairs. Benny crawled into the cabin and flopped on the floor. Dick and Jane were sound asleep, though the light was on. Josh checked their color and saw their rosy cheeks.

"Benny, I need to get your clothes off," Josh said. He was missing one shoe and his thick, black hair was caked with sand. Josh pulled Benny's sopping pants and shirt off, toweled his hair, and rolled him like a carpet in two blankets laid on the floor. With the exception of Mark's family, Josh hadn't had any visitors in months. Now, there were two strangers and a Platé sleeping in his cabin. Josh was worried about the jet skiers and needed reinforcements since he was tapped out, so he grabbed his truck keys from the laundry basket and did a last second check of his guests. Benny got propped on his side in case he puked again, a towel shoved under his head, and a knit cap pulled down to his eyebrows.

The truck roared up the driveway and Josh was off to find cell service for a 911 call. He drove three miles before connecting and sharing the details to the operator. On the drive back to the cabin, the weight of the evening descended.

In the bathroom, Josh reached for the Prozac container from the medicine cabinet. He tried to open it but his vibrating hand made it impossible. Perspiration erupted on his forehead and he leaned on the sink. Josh set the Prozac back in the cabinet; he'd fix this without meds. He owed this to himself and Nate. Shutting his eyes, he drew a deep breath through his nose, and his diaphragm expanded as if he was ready to plunge under water. After several minutes of focused breathing, he remembered his guests in the cabin.

Benny snored in his swaddle of blankets and the kids were conked out. Josh trudged upstairs, leaving a pile of wet clothes behind him, before collapsing in bed. In the depths of a turbulent dream, an artillery shell landed directly on Nate, his best buddy from boot camp at Fort Jackson. They hadn't gone fifty yards from their armored personnel carrier when Josh was heaved backwards from the blast. Nate was only fifteen feet in front of him, and how he died and Josh survived was one story spooling endlessly in Josh's brain.

"Mister, it's morning," said Dick, who was gently tapping Josh's shoulder. Jane was beside him, wrapped in a blanket. "We need to get home or our parents are going to freak."

"Did you find our friends?" Jane said. "We're really worried about them."

KEN POST · 165

From the bed, Josh looked at them, convinced the jet skiers had drowned in the lake. There's no good way to break bad news to kids so young, who have likely never experienced loss. It unnerved him and hit harder than expected. He looked at Dick and Jane. "I'm afraid I—no, I didn't find them." It hurt to say those few words.

The words at Nate's parents' house hadn't come any easier as he shared the last few minutes of Nate's life. They wanted the straight skinny from Josh, who had been 'there' at the end. He spared them the gory detail of finding Nate's headless half-torso riddled with shrapnel.

Jane's sobbing snapped Josh back to his cabin as she leaned on Dick's shoulder. Dick enveloped her in his arms.

Josh rose slowly from his bed, his body as heavy as the memory of a platoon hike with Nate after completing twenty-five miles with an eighty-pound pack. Shoulder to shoulder, spurring each other on. "C'mon," Josh had chided Nate, "We don't want old Ass Pucker (their drill sergeant) giving us latrine duty if we don't keep up." He sat back on the bed to gather his thoughts.

"Are you okay?" Dick asked.

"Gimme a minute. I'll be fine," Josh said. In the back of his mind, he asked if he'd ever be fine.

Josh stood and put a hand on each of their shoulders. "You should head out so your parents don't worry." He reached into his pants on the floor and produced his truck keys, holding them out. "Take these," Josh said. "Can you find your way back here afterwards to drop it off?"

"I think so," said Jane as she took the keys. She wiped her eyes on the blanket.

"Look for the wooden sign with 'Putnam' on it."

On the way downstairs, Dick turned to Josh. "Thanks, Mr. Putnam."

The truck crunched up the driveway and Josh headed downstairs. Benny was cooking bacon and eggs with a bath towel draped around his middle. His clothes hung over a line on the porch to dry.

"Make yourself at home," Josh said as he plopped into a chair at the kitchen table. Now, he had a Platé making him breakfast, topping off a bizarre twelve hours.

"I was wondering when you were going to get up." Benny gestured to the food. "Hungry?"

The mention of food and the aroma hit, and Josh's stomach gurgled. They sat at the table and quietly ate their food.

The toaster popped and Benny got up. "Want a piece?" He buttered a slice, and handed it to Josh like they had known each other for years.

Which, Josh guessed, they had. Just not like this. "Benny, what were *you* thinking?"

He sighed and sipped his coffee, fidgeting with a napkin. "I knew those kids were out there. My boat motor wasn't working so all I had was the canoe. I found one kid floating in the lake, and when I tried to help him, he capsized the canoe trying to get in."

Josh saw Benny looking out the window over his shoulder, to the lake, where several boats droned. Probably Search and Rescue divers looking for bodies. Josh didn't look, afraid he'd witness a dead jet skier getting yanked out of the lake.

"Next thing I know," Benny said, "I'm hanging on to a boat cushion for dear life." A tear formed at the corner of his eye and he flicked at it with a finger. "Between the rain and dark, I never saw that kid again."

"I'll take care of the dishes, Benny," Josh said, and scraped egg remnants from the frying pan into the trash. "You probably want to get home."

"You know, my name is Benoit. B-E-N-O-I-T." His dark eyes looked directly at Josh. It was not a challenging stare. "Benoit Platé," he declared.

"I do know that. I've known it my whole life." Josh liked Benoit's name, the way it rolled off his tongue. "Well, *Benoit,* why don't you take my boat back to your place. You can bring it back later." Josh walked out to the beach next to his dock and bailed the half-filled boat.

Benoit grabbed a bucket from the porch and helped bail. "Thanks for the shoes," Benoit said.

Josh looked at the running shoes he'd lent him since Benoit's shoe disappeared in the previous night's chaos. "Keep 'em, if you want."

At the funeral two weeks later, the church overflowed and Josh slid into a pew near the back. Pictures of the two jet skiers were on the side of the altar, surrounded by multiple bouquets of carnations. An organist played, and a few minutes later he noticed Benoit leaning against the back wall.

After the service, Josh worked his way past a freshly mowed church yard filled with sobbing kids and parents hugging their children. Benoit motioned Josh aside with a nod of his head. "I got beer at my place," he said. "Let's go."

Josh had never crossed the threshold of a Platé house, and it was an odd notion to consider it, let alone be asked to do it.

Benoit stepped into the dark-paneled house and Josh followed him into the kitchen. Pulling two beers from the fridge, they went back outside and parked themselves in chairs overlooking the lake. Josh hadn't had a beer in months, and he paused before twisting the cap. He allowed himself one for good behavior.

"How are you doing?" Benoit said.

"What do you mean? Josh asked.

"You know—" Benoit nodded toward the lake.

"Better, I guess. We did everything possible." There was no use in beating himself up when things happened beyond his control. Josh needed to keep reminding himself of that, and leave the scar tissue alone.

Benoit rose from his seat and walked to the shore, and Josh trailed him to where his canoe, retrieved from the lake, was overturned on the dock. He tapped the canoe with a hand. They both swept their eyes around the lake, as if the jet skiers were going to appear any minute, zooming by, and waving to them.

"Those kids," Benoit's eyebrows furrowed. "What were *they* thinking?" He put his hand up to shield against the glare. "Look at your cabin across the lake," Benoit said. "I bet it looks a lot like my place from your side."

Josh stared at the dark expanse of water toward the green band of pines.

Benoit tipped his beer, they clinked bottles, surveying their domain in silence. Josh listened for the waves but there was only the gentle lap of water.

ASHES

Roy parks on the side of the road with his hands gripping the steering wheel, deciding whether to enter. It isn't because he doesn't know the way. He's been here many times before. After all, he spent much of his childhood playing on this farm where his grandparents lived. Chickens scrabbled at the feed he threw them. He stood tall on a ladder to pluck apples and drop them into a sack looped over his shoulder. Games of hide-and-seek and capture-the-flag in the orchard and pasture. And poison ivy. Lots of it.

The gravel driveway is flanked by two cemented rock pillars. Roy flicks his blinker and turns into the driveway, rocks crunching under his tires. Just beyond the entrance is a sign on a tree with orange neon letters declaring 'No Trespassing.' He continues past the sign, craning his neck to see if anyone is watching. The road dips over a low rise and he eases into a large gravel parking area next to the main house. Roy frowns at the shin-high unmowed lawn—must be an acre of it—leading downhill to the fringe of woods. Two stumps from the old oaks protrude from the ground.

Fifteen or twenty years? Roy isn't sure when he last visited the farm. The old house still needs a paint job, although it is now blue paint peeling instead of white. Down a spur road the old hay barn has toppled over, the roof settled on a pile of broken siding. Farther on, the apple orchard is a tangle of dead limbs and grass up to the crotch of the trees.

Roy unbuckles his seatbelt, steps from the car, and scans the area. He hears a beeping sound and realizes the day-time running lights are still on. He reaches inside the door and turns them off. He can't tell if anyone is home and walks down the flagstone sidewalk to the front door. An old gray F-150 pickup is parked alongside the house. He lifts the brass door knocker—the same one has been on the house for decades—and claps it three times on the door. The house echoes empty and deep. Nothing.

Taking it as a sign to look around a bit more, Roy walks past the truck toward the back of the house. A rotten pile of firewood sits next to a central air conditioning unit and a stack of plastic lawn chairs.

"Can I help you?"

Roy turns to the front of the house where the man must have emerged. He guesses the man must be at least a decade older, gangly, with a sparse gray beard, and reading glasses parked on his forehead.

"I heard you knock, but I was in the basement and couldn't get to the door quick enough."

"Sorry to trouble you." Roy notices the man's pants sagging without a belt.

"Well now that you troubled me, what is it you need?" The man leans on the tailgate of his truck with his arms crossed.

"Excuse me, I should have introduced myself, I'm Roy." He extends his hand.

The man remains motionless, his gaze fixed on Roy. "Well now that you troubled me, *Roy*, what is it you need? You did see the no trespassing sign you drove past, didn't you?"

For a moment, Roy wants to say, 'What sign?' "Yes, I saw the sign."

"But you're still here."

"Well, I need to talk to the landowner. Is that you?"

The man stiffens and stands away from the truck. "You with the government?"

Roy senses the conversation getting away from him. "Ha, no, I'm not with the government. I'm just an insurance agent."

"Don't need no insurance."

"No, no. That's not what I meant. That's what I do for a living; it's not why I'm here.

"Well, get on with it then."

"If you're the landowner, I need your permission."

"Permission? For what?"

"I need your okay to scatter my parent's ashes on your property." It seems like all the air in Roy's lungs expels at once and he feels himself gasping.

"What the hell? I'm gonna call the cops." The man turns toward the house.

Roy raises his voice. "You know, my mom was raised on this farm, and my dad married her here." An old conversation with his father comes to mind. Dad showed up at one of the many social gatherings at the farm, usually coinciding with putting a new roof on the barn, cider-making, or jacking up the foundation of one of the many outbuildings. He saw Roy's mother and knew he wanted to marry her.

Dad said she was wearing overalls and shoveling cow shit and nobody ever looked better doing it.

They celebrated their wedding on a June day outside under the canopy of several large oak trees, just two hundred yards down that same gravel road. The smell of sumac and apple blossoms must have filled the air—at least that's the way Roy remembers the farm.

"When I was a kid, I ran around every acre of this place." Roy subconsciously rubs his elbow from the time he fell out of an apple tree and sprained it.

The man stops in his track and slowly turns around, his long arms swinging beside him. "What's that have to do with me?"

"This place meant everything to them. It was their last wish to have their ashes scattered together on this farm."

Roy sees his dad on the hospice bed, morphine draining into his vein. His withered, pale head barely indenting the pillow, voice not more than a whisper. "Listen—" He tried to lift his head from the pillow but it fell back. "Remember we want—to have our ashes on the farm. Together." Roy sat with his dad's cool, dry hand, their eyes meeting. The hand gently closed on Roy's, and tears formed in both their eyes. "I promise," Roy said.

"It's been a long time, but the way I heard it, your grandpa cheated half this county at one time or another, including my pa." The old man stopped and searched his memory. "Bad checks, no credit. His word was worth less than all those bounced checks." The man fires the words with such force he wipes a trace of spittle from his mouth. "By the time it all caught up with him, all he had left was this farm. Then the bill collectors come and took it."

Growing up, Roy never knew of his grandfather's debts or how he shafted people like the portly butcher who provided the thick pork chops, the painters in stained coveralls, and the movers who packed the new sofa from Spindler's Furniture Shoppe up the stairs. All he saw was the kind man who took him for ice cream cones and set him on his lap on the riding mower. Later on, from his bedroom or a nearby hallway, he overheard snippets of quiet conversations between his mom and dad—and he sensed they were about Grandpa. Those talks would always end when Roy entered the room.

"I don't think they deserve to have their ashes here, given how my pa and a bunch of others were stiffed."

Roy's face burns with his grandfather's history thrown back at him. It was entirely true; still he didn't want to hear it, especially when all he wanted to do is find a final resting place for his parents. A man's word was the hard currency of life. His grandfather squandered that coinage by overspending, a slow-motion erosion of the farm. Both of his parents lamented the loss of the farm, a pastoral haven in his mom's family for four generations. Roy's anger rises at his grandfather but he checks his despair in the presence of the old man. "After all these years you're holding a grudge against my grandfather? I'm talking about my mom and dad."

"It just don't seem fair that any of your kin should be honored here knowing what your grandpa did. That's just part of it." The man lowers his voice an octave. "I don't want spirits of dead folks hovering around this place. That's what graveyards are for. Don't need no ghouls around here."

Roy stands there looking for some other rationale to use. Not much to say to an old coot who believes in spirits.

"So my answer's 'no' if that's what you're wondering."

"I wish you'd see this differently."

"Seems pretty clear to me. I'll see to it to call the cops if you don't leave." He fumbles for his cell phone, searching his pockets. "Now where's that damn phone?"

"Alright, alright. I'm going."

The man follows, twenty paces behind, until Roy is in his car. Roy heads toward the pillared entrance and sees the man in his rear-view mirror, striding up the driveway, as if to usher him and his family history from the farm.

"How'd it go?" His wife, Sonia, is grading math tests at the kitchen table for her high school algebra class. A Diet Coke at her elbow. "Any luck?"

"Zero. The guy is a real asshole." Roy flops on the sofa in the living room across from his wife. Their cat, Mystery, sidles up to the sofa and jumps on it. Roy sets it on the floor.

"So, what happened?" Sonia shoves a pile of paper to one side and turns toward Roy. "What'd the guy say?"

Roy relays his visit to the farm but before he can finish, the cat jumps back on the sofa. Roy plops it back on the carpet. "Can you do something with this cat?"

Sonia walks over, grabs the cat and deposits it outside. "Better?"

Roy sits up. "I wasted a Saturday morning talking to a guy who believes in ghosts. Ashes creep him out. Plus, he's got it in for my grandfather because of all the debt he had—he never even met the guy." He walks over to the sink, grabs a tumbler from the cabinet, heads to the fridge icemaker and two ice cubes drop in the glass. "Then he threatens to call the cops."

"Cops? Why'd he do that?"

"I told you he was a real asshole."

Sonia stands leaning against the fridge, soda in her hand. "What's Plan B?"

"My parents didn't give me one."

"What about the county park your parents liked? You know—Mason Hills—that might be a good spot."

"The one where all those dogs run around illegally off-leash?" Whenever he and Sonia go to the park, one of them always scrapes bonus material off their shoes. "With my luck, they'd be peeing or shitting all over my parents. No way." Roy returns to the sofa and hunches over, massaging his temples with his fingers.

He heads upstairs and yells from the top of the landing. "I'm gonna lay down for a bit." Sitting on the bed, he slips off his shoes and stretches out diagonally across the mattress. He tosses around in his mind how he could have approached the man differently. Maybe he shouldn't have walked around the back of the house without permission. Did that make him look suspicious? Perhaps he should never have asked in the first place and just scattered their ashes. That would have been a lot simpler.

A photo on the wall shows Roy with his parents at his college graduation. No siblings surround him at this big moment. There are none. Mom and Dad's arms are around him, flanking in case he needs protection. All his life he felt that way.

Roy lies on his stomach and tries to fall asleep. He switches to his side propped by a small pillow, and then again to his back, trying get comfortable. His eyes fall on the twin urns sitting on the bookshelf across the room. What kind of son fails a simple deathbed wish?

The next weekend, Roy finishes mowing the back and front yard and perspiration drips down his face. He pulls a red bandana from his back pocket and wipes the sweat from his brow. The tumbler of iced tea Sonia set for him on the patio picnic table is almost empty. He stares out at his lawn, thinking about the expanse of green at the man's house where he wanted to spread his parents' ashes. Sonia slides the screen door aside and steps on to the patio. "Want another iced tea?"

"Nah, I'm good."

"You look lost."

"I guess I'm in a funk." Roy tips back the last of the iced tea and crunches the remains of an ice cube in his teeth. He stares ahead at their neighbor's hedgerow.

"It's that old man, isn't it?" Sonia puts her arm around him. She knows what makes him tick better than a Swiss watchmaker.

"Him and that damned farm." Roy had been wracking his brain for alternative places for the ashes, but nothing felt right. It couldn't just be anywhere; he wanted a place with memories attached: walking down the farm's trail to the small spring in October when the starry sweet gum leaves blazed, eating fresh peach cobbler on the patio picnic table. It feels like a rogue radio station has commandeered his personal airwaves, and keeps playing "Dust in the Wind." He can't shake the tune from his head.

Two days later Roy lies in bed staring at the ceiling, Sonia quietly breathing beside him. His cell phone shows 3:11 a.m. The image of the farm's 'No Trespass-ing' sign burns into the plaster above him. When his grandparents owned the farm, everyone was welcome and nobody needed permission to do anything. You came, you worked, you ate, you laughed, maybe drank too much, and you went home. An hour passes and his appetite kicks in so Roy gently lifts the covers and pads downstairs to the kitchen. He drops a slice of wheat bread in the toaster, dawn creeps in, and he hears birds twitter through the open window. As a kid roaming the farm, he'd always get up early, and he was greeted by the drumming of woodpeckers on apple trees, and warblers trilling from the blackberry thicket.

The toast pops up and Roy eats it slowly in the dark as sleepiness fogs him. Not wanting to wake Sonia, he grabs a quilt from the closet and lays on the sofa bed in the guest room. Mystery leaps on the bed and burrows beside him. Roy reaches out for the purring cat and tells it, "Don't tell anyone, but I've got a plan."

The Fourth of July is a week past and the sun is down. Roy figures by the time he drives an hour, night will have fully settled.

Sonia follows him out to the car in shorts and a tank top, the lingering heat from the day only now starting to fade. In the passenger seat is a daypack. "Don't do anything crazy."

Roy slides into the driver's seat and shuts the door. "I don't intend to. I'm a mild-mannered insurance agent, not James Bond."

"Maybe I should go with you. Be a lookout or something." The window is down and her hand lingers on the door.

"You'd just make twice as much noise or I might lose track of you in the dark. Let's just keep this simple—I'll be back before you know it."

"Okay, I'll stay here in case I have to bail you out."

"Ha-ha. Very funny." One thing Roy appreciates is Sonia's unflappability. She plows ahead with a mathematician's certainty of two plus two equals four. He loves her all the more knowing that trait is wrapped in her gallows humor. Sonia re-enters the house and the outside porch light comes on, sending skeletal rhododendron shadows on the lawn.

Roy turns the headlights off as he steers the car to the shoulder. Before leaving his house he flicked the dome light switch so it doesn't come on when he opens the door. The calendar he consulted showed no moon tonight, and the humid murk envelopes him. Only a distant glimmer of light comes from a streetlight two hundred yards down the road and the nearest house is a quarter-mile away.

He gently shuts the car door and walks past the driveway's stone pillars, switching on a pen flashlight. The narrow red beam provides barely enough light to see where he places his feet. He hasn't worn the old Nike running shoes since—he does some quick math—it must have been when he ran the charity 5k for Alzheimer's research four years ago. His North Face backpack holds two coffee can-size urns with ash, carefully wrapped in old rags to muffle any rattle.

He moves slowly, not wanting to inadvertently kick any gravel in the driveway. It is so dark he can barely see the edge of the driveway. As he nears the house, Roy steers wide in case there are motion detector lights. He feels pine cones under his feet now that he is well off the driveway, and knows he is among the large white pines at the far side of the parking area. Carefully, he picks his way through the pines so he doesn't trip or step on any of the branches littering the ground. The smell of resin fills the air, mingling with the sweat clinging to his tee shirt.

A light is on behind dark curtains on the second floor. Are there any windows open? He can't tell but remembers the air conditioning unit. Anyone running it would have the windows shut on such a hot night. Roy wonders if he should have come in the fall or winter when it would be better for sneaking around. Eyes adjusting to the dim, the faint outline of the man's truck is visible, now parked in the front of the house.

He steps on the uncut lawn, the grass several inches high, and makes his way across it. When he reaches the far end of the lawn near the edge of the woods by the oak stumps, he pauses and listens for several seconds before unshouldering the pack. Stopping to listen again, the only sound is his breathing. He sets the pack on the ground, slowly opening the zipper, and removes the two urns.

The magnitude of what he's about to do hits him, and he remains kneeling with the cans at his feet. All his life his parents were with him, first in the flesh, and then sitting on his bedroom shelf while he contemplated parting with the ashes. The time has come yet he is strangely unprepared to deal with it. The loss of the physical connection overwhelms him, and his eyes moisten and tears drop on the lid of his mom's urn. He momentarily contemplates packing the urns up and going back home.

Roy reminds himself: This isn't about me.

Fortified, he gets up and grabs his mom's urn and unscrews the top. Despite all his planning, he never had the nerve to open the urns until now and hadn't thought about how to actually dispose the ash. Do you bend over and gently place the ash? Hold it waist high and let it filter down? It's not like there's a manual for this kind of thing.

He decides on a low-crouch sprinkle, careful not to let the ash visibly pile up in any one spot. He sets his mom's empty urn down and grabs the other one, intermingling their ash so they are together for eternity. Finally, it's done; he can see the ash in the grass but it's not so obvious it will be visible unless someone walks directly on it before the next rain. Relieved, Roy exhales before setting both urns back in the pack and zipping it up.

"Hey, who's out there?"

Roy stands still, caught in the high beams from a vehicle illuminating the lawn from the parking area near the house. It is like he is in a World War II prisoner of war movie where the Nazi search lights spot the captured Allied soldiers red-handed digging a tunnel. He shields his eyes from the blinding light.

"It's me."

"Who's me?" The vehicle owner shouts.

Roy recognizes the hardness of the old man's voice but can't see anyone in the glare. "It's Roy."

A moment passes as the old man parses his memory. "Roy? Don't know no Roy."

"We met a few weeks ago."

"The insurance guy with the ashes?"

"The same."

A man enters the shaft of light and approaches. He stops, ten feet away. Stained chino pants—zipper open, partially buttoned flannel shirt with cutoff sleeves, and worn loafers with no socks indicate a hurried dressing. "What the hell are you doing out here?"

"Scattering my parents' ashes."

"What the fuck? I thought I told you to get lost."

"You did."

The man seems puzzled by the response as if he misheard Roy's answer. "You don't seem like a very bright insurance agent to me."

"I'm actually quite good at it."

"I told you to never come back here. You're trespassing, know that?" The man moves a few feet closer, backlit by a spectral glow. Moths flit and appear ablaze.

Roy doesn't acknowledge his question.

"You heard me, didn't you?"

"Yes, I did."

"So where are the ashes?"

Roy shuffles carefully along the grass. "Pretty much where we're standing."

"Right here?" The man demands. He moves a few steps closer.

"Yes."

The man tromps roughly across the ground, kicking at the grass. Small puffs of ash rise from grass. "Here's what I think of people who don't respect private property." Ash, suspended in the light, floats in a cloud around them. "Now get the fuck off my property or I'll call the cops." The man brandishes a cell phone in one hand.

Roy sees his parents swirling in the puffs of ash, their last sacred wish violated. Sparks of memory flicker in a deep recess of his brain and burst into flame, pulsing with adrenalized force. He lunges, and in the same motion his fist swings into the man's jaw. The man hits the ground and the cell phone launches into the air. Roy's entire body throbs, a stabbing pain in his knuckle, as he glowers over the man.

Roy's breath comes in gasps. "You piece of shit. My parents' dying wishes—you fucked it all up. My last memory of them is of you walking all over, disrespecting them."

The man lays crumpled, holding his jaw and moaning. A trickle of blood dribbles from the corner of his mouth. Unintelligible words wheeze out. He tries to speak again, chest rising, then lays silent.

"We're good here now, right?"

The man turns his head to him slowly and just coughs.

"Good, right?" Roy repeats.

The man looks up at Roy, his eyes half shut, and nods his head.

The cell phone sits at the edge of the light. Roy walks over to it and nudges it with his foot into the blackness, out of view in case the man decides to call the cops. He picks up his backpack and walks past the man still lying on the ground, one leg now bent at the knee. "You might need some health insurance."

Roy follows the headlight beam back to the vehicle and places the pack on the hood. He opens the truck door and turns off the headlights. Darkness swallows the farm as he trudges up the gravel drive. The previous three minutes of his life play back in a loop. It's as if an unknown inner demon was released, severing this last link to the farm forever. Roy's family doesn't belong to this place anymore, but he kept his word—and in the end, it is all that matters. Roy almost turns back to help the man but the bitter tang of the man's thoughtless act lingers.

At the head of the driveway, Roy pauses at the stone pillars. He opens the backpack and wipes down each urn with a rag, sets an empty urn on top of each pillar and drives off into the night.

THE TURTLE THIEF

S tan slid the tiny HD card into the computer drive and waited for the images from his remote wildlife camera to appear on his screen. It was part of a ritual he had performed for many years: viewing pic after pic, part of the monitoring for the threatened wood turtles he had studied for almost three decades. Most of the photos were triggered by a bird alighting on a branch, a deer gingerly crossing the creek, or the occasional meandering of a raccoon.

The next image propelled Stan from his chair. A man carrying a burlap sack emerged from the thick brush across from the camera as he studied the banks and water. In the time Stan had been observing this turtle population he'd never seen another person, probably because he'd picked a spot far off the road, dense with vegetation. It was pristine habitat; no candy wrappers, empty beer cans, or old tires. This interloper intruded on Stan's space, a guarded sanctuary and private Eden, with clear water sparkling in the slanting rays of the sun.

The man wore dark work gloves and grabbed the brush, sometimes dropping to his hands and knees and peering underneath. Stan held his breath, focusing on the burlap bag. Was it weighted with one of his turtles? Studying the photos frame by frame, Stan noted the date and time on the image as the man moved through the field of view. The man disappeared for a few minutes before reappearing on the opposite bank, and then faded into a wall of brush around a bend.

Had Stan been followed? He had always hidden his tracks and changed his route so a trail would be less visible. Stan never drove his Fish and Game vehicle to the study site for fear of telegraphing his research. He'd park his beat-up Subaru Forester at different locations along the roadside, never too near the small bridge the creek ran under. Even the metadata for his photo locations had been scrubbed to make it impossible to find his site.

It was sad it had come to this; turtle researchers needing CIA skills to evade poachers. It hadn't always been this way. When Stan started out, wood turtles were more numerous along streams or rivers, and you never looked over your shoulder. One thing Stan knew for sure: the thief would be back.

This was personal—the thief was not only destroying Stan's research; he was plucking turtles faster than they could be studied or repopulate. The removal of a few breeding pairs of turtles that didn't reach sexual maturity until fifteen years of age decimated a stream's population.

Did the thief know this? Did he care?

People assumed there would always be more turtles. Extinction chilled Stan to his core. It was final, the end of the line, an evolutionary dead end to a path that went back millions of years. The notion of a gene pool receding into a Darwinian abyss urged Stan on—there must be *one* more thing he could do to prevent it. Late at night he'd awaken and stare at the ceiling, aware of the vacant spot in the bed. His wife, Diane, had passed away three years ago after a protracted battle with breast cancer. With Jake and Lily out of the house, it was now just him and his wood turtles—*Glyptemys insculpta*, with a stunning brown, sculpted carapace, and orange legs. Long thought to be among the most intelligent of turtles, they completed laboratory mazes almost as fast as rats.

Lily pulled him aside one time when she was home for the weekend. "Dad," She put a hand on Stan's arm, "you need to get a life." Lily pointed to the turtle photos on the fridge, walked to the stack of research papers pushed to one side of the kitchen table, and disappeared into the bathroom. She returned with a magazine in her hand. "Who reads the *Journal of Herpetology* on the pot? See what I mean? It's everywhere—you can't walk five feet without tripping over turtle stuff."

Stan snatched the journal from her hand and forced a smile.

"Your life is out of balance." She turned on the faucet, ran water into a glass, and took a long sip. "It hurts to say this with Mom gone only a few years, but you may need a girlfriend."

Then Stephanie showed up.

For four years, Stephanie and Stan were a research team, traipsing through meadows, wading thigh-deep creeks, and tangling with blackberry thorns. It didn't take many trips into the woods together before conversations strayed into academics, religion, politics, and relationships. On occasion, she'd mention an old boyfriend and he'd poke around the periphery, curious if she was dating someone. Stan wondered who his competition was.

"I've had a few boyfriends—things just didn't work out," she said.

"Why's that?" Stan was curious about her current status but always steered clear of delving too far into that realm. He was keenly aware of any perception of sexual harassment. A colleague in a different department had recently lost his job after making what a review board deemed as 'untoward' comments to a coworker.

"I don't know. Maybe it was me." She shook her head and laughed. "I kinda go down a lot of intellectual rabbit holes, and they either didn't want to follow or I was hiding. Deliberate?" She shrugged her shoulders. "Possibly."

There was an opening—sort of. Stan loved his work—his turtles—too much to take any chances. Still, the world was filled with *what ifs*. There were too many *ifs* in life and Stan wished he could strike the word from the English language. All *ifs* had done was ruin people. His professional reputation meant everything. Did it make sense to toss that away on what people would think of as a fling? It wouldn't be a fling in Stan's mind. He'd want it to stick. Stan felt like a wild animal in a trap, its only recourse to gnaw a leg off to escape.

"Look, there's one." Steph pointed to a turtle half-covered by leaves and brush. She plucked him from his hiding place. It was a scorching July day and Stan stood over Steph, glancing at the tiny droplets of sweat arrayed on her smooth skin and tanned shoulders as she placed a caliper on the turtle's shell to measure it. "He's a beaut." The sweat on her neck pooled and glided between her shoulder blades as she epoxied the tiny GPS unit on the turtle. Their eyes met when he held the turtle, while Steph drew blood samples into a syringe.

It wasn't lust that moved him. It was the day-to-day camaraderie, the laughter, head-down concentration, and the devotion to their work. It was Steph's quick snort when she was amused, or her furrowed brow when digging into new data.

Was this a crazy midlife male fantasy of his? He didn't want a red Corvette, or a tricked-out fishing boat. Stan wanted *simpatico*, a melding of the minds, a person who grasped the importance of his work.

Steph had also learned to hide her tracks into the woods and check for anyone suspicious.

Over lunch by a creek, Steph said, "It's pathetic we have to play these games to stay ahead of the poachers." She bit into her hoagie sandwich with more ferocity than usual. "If we catch one, we should string him up by his nuts." A chunk of hoagie fell out of her mouth, landing on the paper wrapper in her lap. She chuckled at her table manners and carried on: "Or maybe the poachers should be marched into the woods and shot."

Stan listened silently, too aware of all the turtle-napping. Not just wood turtles, but other species along with snakes and amphibs. It infuriated him to find a stream without his beloved Woodies in it, and their absence also flushed years of research down the toilet.

The letter from Costa Rica sat on Stephanie's office desk.

"Aren't you going to open it?" Stan asked.

"I'm too nervous." She flicked her hands as if she was shaking water from them. "You do it."

Stan cut the envelope flap with his pocketknife and read the letter. "You got the job." A swelling pride expanded in Stan, followed by a deflation he didn't want to show: grief at losing her. He was elated for Steph; she had toiled for her PhD and spent four overcaffeinated years struggling to keep the academic and work candle flickering. As indispensable to his research as Steph was, she filled a bigger gap in his life, and the looming void appeared cavernous.

Stephanie jumped into Stan's arms and hugged him. "Pura vida, baby!"

He wanted to embrace her longer but the office was not the place for it. "I'm proud of you." It sounded more fatherly than he wanted.

Steph dropped her arms to her side and frowned at the reality of her new job. "Ya know, I'm gonna miss this place. You too, Turtle Man." She let out a long sigh and reached out for another hug.

Screw the office. Stan needed that hug as much as she did. They couldn't fire him for a hug he didn't initiate. "Hey," Stan said. "Let's go celebrate at Pazzoli's with an extra-large everything-on-it, super-duper pizza."

"Beer's on me." Steph pulled a ball cap low on her head and grabbed the car keys.

A month later she was working at a non-profit in Costa Rica managing sea turtle nesting. Stan's bottled-up feelings fizzed. There were no more *ifs*. Her emails trickled in although she might as well have moved to the moon. Each one was a small reminder of the possibilities. Like taking a pebble and putting it on a tombstone as a remembrance.

Steph's small desk space in Stan's office was cleared out except for a few turtle pictures taped to the wall. He didn't have the heart to take them down. Where they used to sit side-by-side in Stan's car parked near the creeks with laptops open, he now slouched in his seat by himself. He stared out the bug-smashed windshield before turning the ignition on.

After a long day in the field, and thick with sweat and grime, Stan checked for ticks and jumped in the shower. He plucked a missed tick inching toward the tattoo, and flicked it into the stream of water, enjoying its swirl down the drain. A leftover Costco roast chicken in the fridge greeted him when he opened the door. Stan lay in bed, his reading glasses perched on his head, watching the numbers on the digital clock slide from minute to minute. Silence: it can fill a room and squeeze all the oxygen out. He dragged the thin quilt over him, toggled the 'off' button on the gooseneck lamp on the bedstand, and called it a night.

* * *

The thief's khaki chinos were flecked with dirt and darkened, muddy circles on his knees. A ball cap, pulled low on his head, made it difficult to see his face. Stan zoomed in on a few pics to read the letters on the hat but they remained indistinguishable. The man was clean shaven, average build, and appeared to be in his late thirties or early forties. There had been vague reports of one or more poachers operating in this part of the state but nothing concrete. Did this guy care about what he was doing? Was the money that important? Stan would have handed him his credit card to prevent the poaching.

It sickened him to think of his turtles with their legs duct-taped and tossed in a mailing box headed for Asia, only to be cooped up in a tiny aquarium. They weren't commodities to be bought and sold; they were priceless animals who existed long before man walked the planet and claimed it for his own.

* * *

Stan walked over to the building next to his office where the fish and wildlife enforcement staff worked.

"I got something for you, Mike," Stan said.

A thick-waisted man with unruly blond hair looked up from a pile of papers. The wire rack on one side of his desk was crammed with thick files, and yellow sticky notes plastered his computer monitor. "Hold on a sec. I gotta write something down before I forget." Mike scribbled on a pad. "Okay, what can I do for you?"

Stan handed him the jump drive.

Mike plugged the drive into his computer and watched the video. "Game cam, right?"

"Yup."

Mike replayed the short video clip a few times, pausing it twice to take a closer look. "What's in his bag?"

"It's empty. He's looking for wood turtles. He's gonna wipe 'em out if we don't catch him."

"What else ya got?"

"That's it. Does this guy look familiar?" Stan said.

"Nope." Mike held the jump drive up. "Can I keep this?"

"Sure. It's your copy."

Mike stuck a piece of tape on the drive labeled "wood turtles" and dropped the drive into an empty coffee mug.

Stan noticed several other drives in the cup with other species' names on them. "What do you think?"

"I see a white male, mid-to-late 30s or early 40s with a burlap bag next to a creek. Could be digging mushrooms. Least, that's how a judge would see it."

"Mike, he's not digging mushrooms and you know it."

"Easy, Stan, easy. Just playing devil's advocate." Mike rolled back in his chair. "We'll keep an eye out but if you can get a good face shot, a clear view of this guy stuffing turtles into that bag, a license plate number or whatnot, then we'll have more to work with. Right now, Mr. Wood Turtle Thief is just a face in a crowd." Mike spread his arms in front of his desk. "Unfortunately, I've got a ton of other assholes I'm trying to find."

A dryness in Stan's throat welled up.

"Keep me posted, and thanks," Mike said.

Stan crossed the parking lot back to his office. It was time to do his own sleuthing and take care of this himself.

Stan no longer focused solely on his turtles—he wanted the thief. A black veil descended on Stan and all he thought about was harming the man. If he found him, he'd lash him to a tree and let insects feast on him. That would serve the bastard. Pistol-whip him while he was on his knees begging for his life? Make him feel tangible pain. Stan was treading a path he had never been down. Was the man dangerous? What if they encountered each other in the woods? Stan snapped on a light in their bedroom walk-in closet and felt for the gun stuffed under his wool sweater on an upper shelf. His fingers closed on the hard metal and he moved to the edge of the bed, palming the Colt 45 passed down to him from his grandfather's time fighting Nazis in Italy. The smooth lines of steel, corrugated grip and smell of gun oil comforted him. In the garage, Stan dropped some extra-long zip ties into his pack along with rope and duct tape. If he encountered the thief, he'd have to subdue him. All options were on the table.

Stan identified the roads bisecting the creek to determine how a poacher might access the area. He installed several new game cameras, staked out his study site, pulling over on the county road as the first rays of sunlight glimmered over the horizon. Stan was careful to remain far enough uphill from the bridge over the creek to surveil the area. Settling into his seat and cradling a thermos of coffee, he'd crack open his laptop and work. Steph used to be in the seat next to him when they'd return from the field, typing up notes and entering data. He reached out and ran his hand over the seat's fabric, as if he was touching her. He strained for any remaining scent of her: the lemon-ginger body wash, her sweat, the hazelnut creamer she dumped in her coffee.

Should he have shared his feelings with Steph? Showed his cards? A dangerous tipping point could ruin a remarkable partnership. Or was he deluding himself, mistaking friendship for a relationship?

Summer passed and the combination of work and spying ground Stan down. He walked down from the bridge buttress and dove into the brush along the creek, his backpack snagging on vines. Two hundred feet into the woods, a cigarette butt lay in the heel of a footprint—someone had been to his site recently. Stan always carried tweezers and Ziploc bags in his field kit and had watched plenty of CSI shows, so he grabbed the butt with tweezers and dropped it into a small Ziploc for potential DNA analysis. Hurrying past ancient oaks and maples dappling sunlight, he wended deeper toward his site. He crossed and recrossed the stream or scampered along a log. Sweat dripped from his forehead and rivulets burned his eyes as he surged forward. Normally, he was slow and deliberate, enjoying the thick smell of the flowering dogwood and sassafras, the sight of slickened turtle basking logs, and the staccato battering of woodpeckers. There was no time for that now.

After thirty lung-searing minutes, Stan hunched over to catch his breath before unfolding his telemetry antenna and holding it aloft, listening for signals. He angled past a patch of poison ivy and skirted a muddy sand bar. The turtle's GPS unit lay in a tangle of high grass; it had been pried off "Martha," a twenty-five-year-old female. "Fuck!"

Switching frequencies on his receiver, he searched for "Randy," a twenty-seven-year-old male with fiery red eyes. There was no signal and he spotted the GPS, submerged in a shallow riffle.

Practically family since being trapped in 1997, both were gone, likely in the thief's burlap sack and on their way to China in a cardboard box. His kids had named both turtles. A tightness gripped Stan's head as if a leather band was cinched tight. His feral scream emanated from a deep trench. Drained, he dropped to the creekbank, boots dangling submerged in the cool water. His turtle tattoo, matching the one Stephanie got with him on a lark, peeked from under his t-shirt sleeve, and he traced a finger along its lines. He had not asked for much from life and it was all drifting away. As Stan sat, the water curled around a root wad, spinning in a circle.

* * *

It was mid-morning when a car approached and pulled over a quarter-mile away. Stan slithered in his seat out of sight, slowing rising to peer over the steering wheel. A man got out wearing a small backpack and carrying something in his hands. With his binoculars, Stan thought it was the same guy in his video. What were the odds? *He's getting greedy.* The man looked around and dropped down the road embankment out of sight. Stan tapped a note into his phone with the make and model of the car.

Steadying his breathing, he set a timer on his phone for three minutes to give the man a head start. Approaching the empty car, he snapped photos of the body, license plate, and interior. The advantage was all Stan's: the man didn't know he was being watched, and Stan knew the woods so well he could walk to his study site on a moonless night if he had to.

He eased down toward the stream bank, taking care to keep branches from snapping and brush snagging on him. Stan wished he had Steph at his side, although she was there in spirit. What would she do? Right or wrong, he had let Steph slip away without a word. He wasn't going to make a mistake with a turtle thief; this guy had taken a chunk from his life. He reached into his pack for the Colt and his finger brushed the safety as he tracked the man farther into the woods, unsure if he was able to distinguish what had been stolen and what had been lost.

ENOLA GAY

It was a hot night in late May, and we sat on the sofa watching *All in the Family* when the shouting started next door. A door slammed and the Martins' Ford LTD roared down their driveway. "Don't you ever come back, asshole!" Tires screeched, followed by a pounding on our door so hard I thought the jamb would splinter. We rushed to the door and Enola Gay was breathing hard and could barely speak.

"Come quick, Mom's really hurt. That fucker was drinking again and hit her." Her father's crimson handprint splayed across her face. She fell to the floor sobbing in our entry as my parents dashed to the light green ranch house adjacent to ours.

That fucker was her father: Lieutenant Paul Martin, logistics officer at nearby McGuire Air Force Base. He kept the base organized while his home life unraveled in alcohol and anger. Nobody knew what drove Lieutenant Martin to beat his family but this wasn't the first time. When his wife, Pat, was over at our house drinking tea one winter afternoon, she let on her husband was frustrated because he wanted to be a jet pilot. An abnormal heartbeat kept him out of flight school so he was shunted into logistics when he showed an aptitude for keeping the PX well-stocked and the base's two thousand toilets supplied with paper.

I helped Enola Gay off the floor and got her a glass of water and a tissue. The imprinted mark glowed on her face, so I popped some cubes out of an ice cube tray and wrapped them in a washcloth. She touched the cubes gingerly to her cheek, said "Thanks, Will," and lightly touched my hand.

Dad ran back and yelled, "The phone's ripped from their wall! Call 9-1-1!" He sprinted back to help my mom. The untucked shirt and blood on his pants pocket hinted at what he was dealing with.

* * *

The Martins had moved next door four years earlier. Three bedrooms, one-and-three-quarter baths, and a kidney-shaped built-in pool with a diving board at the deep end. The daughter: Enola Gay, named after the plane that dropped the atomic bomb on Hiroshima—a fact I knew from history class. The son: her older brother, Luke. They were Air Force brats who lived everywhere from Guam to Georgia, and many points in between. Within a month after Luke's high school graduation, he had enlisted in the Air Force, and was stationed in California.

"We want to stay put so the kids can have some stability during high school," Mrs. Martin said when she first came over to introduce herself. My mom and Mrs. Martin became friends, chatting at our kitchen table drinking iced tea in the summer and hot tea in the winter. Mr. Martin kept to himself except on the occasional weekend when a bunch of Air Force buddies showed up with big trucks or sporty cars. They'd convene in the backyard and we'd hear laughter, feet stomping beer cans on the concrete apron surrounding the pool, and smell steaks grilling.

From my backyard I saw Enola Gay stayed away from her father and his friends, sitting at the opposite end of the pool in a lawn chair. Kids at high school gave Enola Gay a wide berth too, despite her good looks. Tall and straight as a stick of dynamite with a thick crop of copper-brown hair. It reminded me of the color of the wire in the small electric motors I took apart to see what made them tick. She was touchy and detonated at school more times than I could count. A third of the girls in school were car-pet-bombed with 'fuck-you's' for snide remarks or staring too long at Enola Gay. The sanctimonious Catholic girls steered clear of her like she was radioactive. A girl on the softball team called her a lesbo loner and was pummeled and left crying in a fetal position under a study hall desk. Enola Gay got a three-day suspension. My hunch is boys were baffled by her or she scared them off. With me, it was different. Maybe because we were neighbors, but I think it was more because I never judged her.

* * *

An ambulance and police car pulled up, red strobe lights bouncing off the houses surrounding the Martins. The Paulinskys across the street, in matching striped robes, watched from their door stoop. My dad held the front door open while the EMTs wheeled a gurney inside. From behind the screen door at our house, Enola Gay, with the chilled washcloth against her face, saw her mom lowered in the ambulance and driven away. She let out a strangled gurgle and I wondered how this was all going to play out.

It didn't take long to find out. Lieutenant Martin had a new home in the McGuire brig and Mrs. Martin was in a private room at the base hospital. Mom pulled the car up near the azaleas in the driveway after returning from the hospital. Enola Gay sat, unmoving, in the passenger seat.

"How is Mrs. Martin?" I asked.

"Not good." Mom said. "She's got a broken nose, split lip, two loosened teeth, a concussion, and laceration on the back of her head needing eight stitches. Doctors think the last two injuries happened when Pat hit the edge of the coffee table before landing on the floor."

Mom walked to the other side of the car and knocked on the window. Enola Gay slowly cranked the window down.

"Are you coming out?" Mom asked.

"I'm gonna stay here awhile."

"Can I get you anything?"

"Nope." Enola Gay stared straight ahead and raised the window.

Mom looked at me and I shook my head, meaning, 'just let her be.'

A half-hour afterward, there was a knock on the door.

"Will, can I talk with your mom?" Enola Gay said.

Mom hunched over a screaming vacuum in the living room. I made a slashing sign by my throat to cut the motor.

The vacuum whirred to a stop. "What is it, Will?"

"Enola Gay wants to talk with you."

"Oh, okay." She took a bandana from a pocket and patted her forehead. Mom stepped out the screen door and she and Enola Gay walked over to the lawn. Through the screen door I saw Enola Gay gesture to her house and then ours. I had never seen Mom and Enola Gay say more than the typical greetings neighbors share. My mom gave her a hug and they parted.

"Well?" I asked.

"Enola Gay's moving in with us for a few days. Until her mom is home. She's gathering some things right now."

Four days later, I was mowing the lawn and the LTD pulled up in the driveway. Mrs. Martin stepped gingerly out of the car and gave a weak wave to me. I turned the mower off and offered to help but she gestured with the flick of a hand she was okay.

"Your mom home?"

"I think she's making dinner."

Her makeup did little to conceal a face clotted with faded purple and yellow blotches. A bluish ring lurked under the left eye. I followed Mrs. Martin into the house and Mom gave her a quiet hug as they moved into the living room.

"Will, can you get Pat some iced tea, please?" My mom adjusted a pillow behind her back on the sofa. "Should I call Enola Gay in? She's out back reading a book."

"In a bit. First, I need to ask a favor of you, Karen. A big one."

"Of course, Pat. Anything I can do to help."

"I was hoping," Mrs. Martin paused for a second, "actually, I was praying you could take care of Enola Gay for longer than a few days—more like a couple months. My mom, bless her heart, is down in Abilene and had a stroke. She'll be in the hospital for a couple weeks but she'll need home care in the worst way, Dad's gone, and my brother's a drunk in Portland." Mrs. Martin, touched her cheek, winced. "Least, last I heard. Not much help coming from him."

Mom sat back on the sofa and rearranged a small cushion behind her back. "I see." A framed needlepoint Quaker saying hung on the wall above her.

You Lift Me and I'll Lift Thee
and We'll Ascend Together

Her surprise gave way to her religion, kicking in at full force. My parents were devoted Quakers and their beliefs centered on peace, freedom of conscience, and 'doing the right thing.' They strived to make the world better and respect each individual. This was an opportunity to help right the damage inflicted by Lieutenant Martin. "Of course, I'll have to check with George (my dad) to make sure he's okay with it."

"With so much going on in Enola Gay's life right now she needs consistency, not change." Mrs. Martin, lifted the iced tea to her lips, sipped. "If I bring her with me to Texas, she has to start all over and I won't even be settled. She doesn't make friends easily and it will be too hard on her."

I counted her friends and arrived at one—me, although I wouldn't say we were good friends—that came later. My older brother, Kyle, off to Michigan State, and I swam in the Martin's pool with Enola Gay and Luke the past few summers. She'd leap like an antelope off the diving board and cannonball me in the water, or try to dunk me while we played tag. I noticed her bikini top needed readjusting when we'd wrestle in the water.

Our friendship evolved over math problems. Enola Gay hated anything with numbers and was close to failing Algebra II. In March of her senior year, right after quarterly grades came out, Mrs. Martin came over with Enola Gay in tow.

"Will, you're really good at math. Would you help Enola Gay with her homework? I can pay you, if you'd like."

"No need to pay me, I've got to do my homework anyway so it shouldn't be much extra work." It was pure bravado since I breezed through math and Enola Gay slogged through it like an infantryman in a Vietnamese swamp. I'd be carrying her through that swamp on my back. I looked past Mrs. Martin's shoulder at Enola Gay to see if she was okay with this arrangement; an unreadable Mona Lisa smile creased her face.

"At the very least, let me bring snacks over for you two during the lessons." Mrs. Martin rubbed her hands together. "I'll make a double batch of brownies to get things started."

We scribbled quadratic equations, polynomials, and logarithms on a pad at our kitchen table almost every day after school, doubling back over them as Enola Gay struggled to learn a language so natural to me, though I was only a junior. I looked forward to the sessions after discovering she had a quick wit and an active mind—a product of books as her best friends. She confided about her taunting at school and loneliness. "It doesn't help that I'm named after the biggest, baddest plane that dropped the A-bomb."

"A lot of kids at school are assholes." I got up and grabbed a bag of chips from the counter. The cliquishness of high school kids stirred me—I wasn't part of the 'in crowd' either—and I scattered crumbs all over the floor while I was eating.

"I'm not stupid like a lot of kids think." She put her pencil down, mid-formula. "I just don't care."

"That's why we're doing this." I returned to the table with the chips. "To show them you are smarter than they think."

Enola Gay looked at me and in typical deadpan fashion, said, "Are you going to share those chips or am I going to have to arm wrestle you for them?"

My tutoring worked. At the end of Enola Gay's final quarter in high school, she rushed over to my house. "Will, I got a C instead of a D-minus. I passed!" She hugged me so hard my ribs hurt. "All because of you!"

During our math sessions I also learned she loved to run late at night.

"It's quiet and my mind can let go," she said. "Only the streetlights know I'm passing by."

* * *

Mrs. Martin turned to my mom. "I can't live in that house, not after what he did to me." She sat for a few seconds, staring into her teacup. "I was a fool to stay married to him. I thought I was doing it for the kids, but that didn't turn out so well, did it?" Tears rimmed her eyes, she plucked a tissue out of her pocketbook, and blew her nose.

I leaned on the wall, shifted uncomfortably, and realized the world of adults was much more complicated than my routine of going to school, hanging out with friends, and watching TV. Our family life was pretty much all-American, but it was clear sunlight did not pour into every household.

My mom patted Mrs. Martin's hand. "What about your house?"

"I'm selling it as soon as I can." A resolute look replaced Mrs. Martin's tears. "The sooner it's gone, the better."

* * *

Enola Gay was out of earshot on the patio reading when Mom broached the subject. She had waited until dessert was finished and Dad's eyes glazed over. "George, what do you think of Enola Gay staying with us longer?"

Dad gathered the last of the apple crisp crumbs on his fork. "How much longer?"

"Until the end of summer, when Pat thinks she'll be settled."

"Hmmm." He puckered his lips and held them there, pondering. "Enola Gay's a bit different, for sure. Where will we put her?"

"She's already in Kyle's room so she might as well stay there. It's not like he's using it while he's in college this summer taking extra classes."

"What if he comes home for a few days?"

"He can sleep in the TV room." Mom got up to put the plates in the dishwasher. "The sofa's big enough for him to sleep on."

"You mean Kyle won't have his own room if he returns?"

"George, he'll survive. Girls need more privacy."

Dad got up, opened the fridge for more milk and sat back down. He shifted in his chair and turned his gaze to me. "What do you think of all this?"

"It could work," I said. "Besides, we swam in their pool the last few years." I wanted to say I liked the way she smelled when we sat elbow-to-elbow doing homework. "She's actually pretty nice when you get to know her."

Mom cut in. "George, the only real inconvenience is you'll have to stop wandering around the house in your underwear."

Dad pushed his plate away and finished the last swig of milk in his glass. His family possessed Quaker roots going back to the 1600s. A stalwart of the religious community, he served many terms as a clerk on various Friends committees. I knew this was his way of processing our new 'family' member. "Well, I guess we can make this work."

* * *

The weeks before school ended in late June, both households scrambled over the impending move. Mrs. Martin worked day and night packing boxes, making trips to the curb with garbage and other detritus from suburban life. The Salvation Army truck pulled up multiple times and I heard the driver declare, "Lady, I can't take no more with this load. I'll be back tomorrow." A real estate agent pounded a 'for sale' sign in the front lawn and couples, some with little kids trailing, began wandering about the Martins' house. "Munchkins," my mom called them. I fretted who my new neighbors would be.

At our house, Mom sanitized Kyle's room by taking down all the hot Stevie Nicks posters, rolling them up, and sliding them into cardboard tubes. His tennis trophies, books, and clothes were carefully boxed, catalogued, and labeled with a red marker before placement in the garage on shelves my dad hastily cobbled together. The sewing machine clattered away as she fashioned new curtains for Kyle's room while we watched TV.

Enola Gay carried laundry baskets filled with clothing from her room and hung it in Kyle's closet, some of which I'd never seen her wear. Nobody was going to mistake her for a spiffy dresser: jeans, cutoffs, tube tops, tee shirts, and peasant blouses were her go-to outfits. She looked good in all of it. No mini-skirts, heels, or other adornments to keep the boys ogling or make friends envious. I guess clothing to her was what you wore to keep from being naked.

My job was helping carry Enola Gay's stuff over, assisting Mrs. Martin with lifting furniture and heavy boxes, and staying out of the way. The bustle excited me but I was also unsure of how this would work. What would dinner conversation be like? Would there be more competition for the family cars? How long would I have to wait for a *girl* to use the bathroom? I wondered what Enola Gay was thinking; in a flash her life was leveled. Her outwardly stoic nature rarely revealed much. On any given day, it was hard to tell if she was flying at 30,000 feet or if her wheels hadn't left the ground. We were a chatty family and this would be a new dynamic for all of us.

On a sultry graduation evening, our backs sweated against the metal chairs aligned in neat rows. People cheered or clapped when the gowned students crossed in front of the stage at the end zone of the football field. They clutched their diplomas flashing peace signs, screaming ecstatically, or walking off with aplomb.

Mrs. Martin searched for Enola Gay's name in the program. "There it is. See it? She did it!"

"Yes, it's wonderful." Mom hugged Mrs. Martin.

Dad patted Mrs. Martin's knee. We knew this day was the product of many skirmishes and quite a few battles. The line of 'Ms' snaked forward and Mrs. Martin, rolled program in hand, tapped it against her thigh.

"Enola Gay Martin," the principal said into the microphone.

Enola Gay, not comfortable in the limelight, slinked forward like a nocturnal animal stealing food from a trap when she received her diploma. The audience was silent until we clapped and Mrs. Martin put two fingers in her mouth and whistled so loud my ear drums popped.

Within two days from graduation, the house sold to a family from Connecticut with two elementary school kids. The 'for sale' got yanked from the ground a few days later. They wouldn't be moving in until right before school started in early September.

Mrs. Martin didn't waste any time after the house sold. The Mayflower moving van sat at the curb fully loaded and the LTD idled in the driveway in the morning sun. We gathered to say goodbye. Mom and Dad hugged Mrs. Martin, and Enola Gay took her turn. They held each other so long it seemed they were riveted together. Enola Gay burst into a paroxysm of crying and Mrs. Martin clung to her tighter, whispering in Enola Gay's ear. She cleared tears from her eyes and Enola Gay's eyes with her forefinger. The car door shut, a heavy thud like a mortar round echoing off the nearby houses. The ignition started and Mrs. Martin sat there momentarily, as if she was going to say something, before backing out, and following the Mayflower truck rumbling down the street. We were now alone with Enola Gay, and she was alone with us.

We were officially on Day One of Summer Break: June 22nd. I was disassembling a small TV I found at the curb down the street on garbage day. Parts were spread on a newspaper on the kitchen table. Mom came back from her part-time office manager job at Granger Home Construction.

"Honey, I asked you to do that on dad's workbench in the garage. You're going to scratch the table."

"The light's better in here."

"This is the last time, Will. Have you seen Enola Gay?"

I nodded over my shoulder to Enola Gay's new favorite place; the patio, laid out on a woven nylon-strapped chaise lounge lawn chair. She was wearing cutoff shorts, a polka dot bikini top, and a pair of large-framed, round sunglasses, too big for her narrow face.

The screen door opened and my mom said, "I think I found a job you might like."

Enola Gay lowered her glasses. "What is it?"

"Sales person at Zales Jewelers."

"Does it require me to smile a lot and be nice?"

My mom sat on the chair next to Enola Gay. "I'm sure that would be an important part of the job."

"I'm not exactly in a smiley, nice frame of mind, right now."

"I see. Give it some time. That might change." The aluminum legs of the lawn chair scraped the patio as my mom rose.

"Maybe." Enola Gay picked up her book and started reading.

A half-hour later, Enola Gay sat down at the kitchen table, placing her book spread-eagle. "Why do you like taking things apart?"

I squinted into the shell of the TV, flashlight in hand, in search of a red wire. Without looking up I said, "I guess I like to figure out how things work."

"Let me see." She reached inside the TV. "Shit!" Enola Gay cut her hand on a sharp piece of aluminum. She pulled her finger out and blood was dripping from below her fingertip.

"Pinch it tight," I directed. I grabbed a napkin and wrapped the fingertip. "Now hold this in place while I get a band-aid."

"Am I gonna live?"

"Not if my mom hears you curse again."

Enola Gay's index fingertip was swaddled with a thick wad of gauze taped over it, staunching the blood flow.

I started cleaning up my electronic mess. "How are you going to pick your nose with that thing on?"

Enola Gay slowly lowered the bandaged finger and raised the finger next to it and left it there. With her other hand, she punched me in the shoulder and it hurt more than I let on. Now I knew why half the school was afraid of her.

"I guess I'll pick my nose with my other hand," she said.

I gestured to the book on the table. "What are you reading, anyway?"

"*Lady Chatterley's Lover*. Have you read it?"

"Heard of it, but haven't read it." I reached for the book, careful not to lose Enola Gay's page. "What's it about?"

"I'm only about halfway through so it's hard to say. I think it's about class struggles, and different types of love—sexual, mental, stuff like that." She took the book from me and thumbed the pages. "It was pretty racy for its time. Got banned and everything."

"I think I'll stick to electronics."

"How boring. Want me to read you the sexy parts?"

Enola Gay cocked an eyebrow at me, flashing that Sphinx-like smile. I wasn't sure what to make of it although a warm feeling came over me from nowhere.

Mom was busy in the kitchen, clattering pans. "William, is that table clear of all your stuff yet? Dad will be home soon."

"I guess we'd better wash up," Enola Gay said.

I watched her walk to the bathroom, the heat in my head slowly subsiding.

My full-time job at Radio Shack started before the Fourth of July. One evening after the Fourth, while we were sitting in the living room eating peanuts, Enola Gay succumbed to my mom's subtle pressure to find a summer job.

"You've got a job, Enola Gay." Mom's contacts in the construction industry found her work in the local plumbing and electrical supply warehouse. "If you want it."

"I don't have to talk to a lot of people, do I?" Enola Gay asked my mom.

"You'll be in the back of the warehouse stocking shelves. So no, I don't think you'll be talking to people aside from Don, the owner, and his two counter people. Of course, you'll have to take the bus each way."

"I can read on the bus," Enola Gay said. "How much does it pay?"

"Three dollars an hour."

"I talked Don into an extra fifty cents an hour because I told him you were strong enough to lift heavy boxes."

"Your pay includes all the plumbing supplies you'll ever need," I chided.

"Shut up!" Enola Gay threw an embroidered pillow at me.

Mom gave Enola Gay a stern look for her bad 'word choice.' "Look at you two, like brother and sister."

For the next two weeks, deep into the swelter of mid-July, work kept Enola Gay and I from seeing much of one another until dinner. In the evening, we'd watch TV, take Tidbit, our dachshund, for a walk around the block, or hang out in our respective rooms. Enola Gay went for her evening runs, only earlier since she had to work the next day. I'd fall asleep to the shower running or catch glimpses of her exiting the bathroom in a tee-shirt damp from wet hair.

One night Mom and Dad had dinner plans so Enola Gay and I stopped at Vinny's Pizzeria. We found a booth near the back, surrounded by wallpaper images of the Roman Coliseum, an aqueduct, and a chariot. I was ready to order the pepperoni special.

"Will, maybe we should skip the pizza."

I looked at Enola Gay, puzzled by her change of heart. "What do you mean? I thought you were hungry—I'm hungry."

Enola Gay looked around the pizzeria. Several high school kids stared at us, two whispering with hands over their mouths. "Depending on my mood, normally I'd either ignore them or tell them to fuck off."

"Are you worried eating a pizza with you will ruin my reputation?" I pushed the menu toward the salt and pepper shakers.

"Kinda." Enola Gay fiddled with a napkin. "I'm not the most well-liked person in school."

"There's a better way to handle it." I preferred a more subtle approach to make the same point. "I'm not going anywhere."

"Are you sure?" Enola Gay looked up from the twisted napkin, our eyes met for longer than normal. I think she realized I had her back.

"Of course, I am. But let's have some fun." I grabbed her hand and led her to an empty booth next to the snickering kids, sliding next to her.

Enola Gay's eyes opened wide. "What are you doing?"

Uncomfortable with our proximity, the kids edged out of the adjacent booth and left the pizzeria.

"So, pepperoni's fine, right?"

By the end of July, the evening routine crystallized on our time off; I'd go visit friends, and Enola Gay turned the outside patio light on to read or she'd watch TV. My friends came by, but usually not for long with Enola Gay around. It was like they tiptoed around a minefield. She'd retreat to her room when they showed up or remain outside on the porch, uninterested in our antics or refrigerator raids. I sensed my friends resented the time I spent with Enola Gay, and I felt badly not hanging out with them as much. I knew better than to tell them I enjoyed her company since they didn't 'get' Enola Gay. I definitely didn't want to tell them I kinda more than liked her. Besides, she was only in town for another month or so.

"Hey, we're going swimming at the quarry tomorrow at two o'clock," Danny, my best friend, said. "Are you coming or is it gonna be another day with EG?"

Stu, never the diplomat said, "Is she your girlfriend, or what?"

I was in full denial mode. "C'mon, give me a break, guys. She's living with us temporarily." I opened up a Tupperware with chocolate chip cookies my mom baked for us. "What am I supposed to do, ignore her?"

Stu wasn't buying it. "Is she jerking you off?"

"SShh. Okay, that's it." I was concerned Enola Gay would hear their chatter which would only piss her off more. They grabbed some cookies and I ushered them out the door, stepped out on the concrete stoop. "I'll see you at the quarry tomorrow."

One Saturday night I came home early, the threat of a thunderstorm rustling the leaves, followed by the distant rumble of thunder. My parents were at a Friends fundraiser Dad orchestrated for Vietnamese orphans. A blue TV glow from the back room flashed so I wandered to the doorway. Enola Gay was stretched out on the sofa like Cleopatra, with a big bowl of popcorn on her lap. Tidbit cuddled next to her, his eyes following each kernel of popcorn heading to Enola Gay's mouth.

"Hey," I said.

"You're back early." She sat up and Tidbit slid off the sofa.

"Nothing really going on." I leaned on the door frame, glancing at an aspirin commercial in the background. My friend Gary's parents had gone to Asbury Park for the night, so we had gathered for a poker game, found someone eighteen years old to buy us a twelve-pack, and smoked a bowl in the backyard. Another night in suburbia. "What are you watching?"

"*Chiller Theater.* Wanna watch?" She scooted over for me.

"Sure. Which movie is it?"

"*The Atomic Man*. Haven't seen this one before."

"What's it about?" I reached over to the bowl and grabbed a handful of popcorn.

"An atomic scientist named Dr. Rayner gets radioactive poisoning that puts him seven seconds ahead in time. He's also got a body double trying to mess up his experiments." She slipped some popcorn to Tidbit sitting on the floor. "The plot's a little confusing."

Enola Gay squinted at me as I shoved in a mouthful of popcorn. "You're high, aren't you?"

I stopped in mid-chew. "Can you tell?" I was far down the path of stoned oblivion feeling invisible to the world.

"Duh." She shifted the bowl back to her lap. "For one thing, you're eating all my popcorn. Plus, your eyes look like slits, and you smell like weed. Call me Sherlock Holmes."

"Does that make me Watson?"

"No, it makes you dufus Inspector Lestrade from Scotland Yard. He couldn't solve a murder if he tripped over the body. Don't worry, I won't tell your parents."

"You think they can tell?" I didn't know what the official Quaker position was on smoking pot, but prudence was in order.

"They're absolutely clueless." She turned back to the TV. "Sshh, it's on again."

We sat shoulder to shoulder, munching popcorn and glued to the TV as Dr. Rayner's radiation diagnosis became clearer. Enola Gay wore a sleeveless tee shirt and I felt her heat, like a warm wave, right through my shirt. The smell of butter and salt filled the room and at one point, both our hands were in the bowl together. She took a piece of popcorn and gently placed it in my mouth. I returned the favor. She took my hand and licked my fingers, her eyes gauging the effect on me. Dr. Rayner's fate was no longer important. Our heads nodded toward each other and we kissed, the world a slow-motion carousel. The pace picked up and when her hand dropped into my lap, the mercury kept rising in my internal thermometer. I fumbled with her bra's clasp.

The front door opened and my parent's said, "We're home!"

In our dash for an aura of presentability, the popcorn bowl went flying, scattering pieces all over the floor for Tidbit, as he vacuumed each kernel.

We both shouted, "We're in here watching TV."

The next few weeks Enola Gay and I smiled at each other, wondering did that really happen? Was it because I was stoned? Did we really like each other that much? Did we *need* to like each other that much to go down that road? It was a weird courtship and our flirtation consisted of glances and innuendo, disguised to throw my parents off the scent. It was invigorating and taboo at the same time. We were supposed to take care of Enola Gay, not take advantage of her. My head was an overheating circuit board and I could barely connect two wires the whole time I was in this trance.

My parents never gave us the chance. Dad's company was bidding on a project and his work exploded with overtime. He brought it home on weekends and evenings, hunched over in his office with his desk light shining on his bald spot. Mom caught a nasty cold which lingered for weeks. They curtailed their social life and Enola Gay and I circled like two cats at the zoo, unsure if we wanted another opportunity or what we'd do if another chance came around.

The last week of August was a blast furnace of heat and humidity. It reminded us of the movie, *The Day the Earth Caught Fire*, we'd watched the week before on *The Late Show*. Enola Gay and I reclined on the lawn chairs on a Saturday night while my parents were at a Friends potluck followed by a show at the local theater. To cool off, we sipped sweating glasses of lemonade parked on the patio next to our chairs. The porch light was off and with no moon, we sat draped in indigo darkness speckled with the occasional flare of a lightning bug.

Enola Gay rummaged next to her chair under a towel, shirt, and book, producing a joint and a lighter. She flicked open the lighter and lit the joint hanging from her lip. "Want some?"

Enola Gay handed it to me—where she got it, I have no idea, and I never asked.

"Sure." I toked, and the glow of my inhale reflected in her face. We smoked the joint until it was a nub I dropped when it burned my fingers. An eternity seemed to pass and the crickets kept getting louder and louder.

"Let's go." Enola Gay stepped away from the recliner.

I was floating in my own world and her words echoed in my head but I was unsure of their meaning. "Go where?"

"Follow me." She marched off across the yard to her old house until she disappeared in the blackness. "Coming?"

I met her at the low chain link fence separating our backyards. "Where are we going?"

Without answering, she clambered over the fence and I could barely discern Enola Gay near her old pool. The house where she spent the last four years lay dark, awaiting its next residents in a week. The concrete apron surrounding the pool sent the day's residual heat rising into the soles of my feet. "What are we doing?"

"Skinny dipping." Enola Gay had already dropped her shorts and underwear in a pile and was taking off her shirt.

I stood immobile for a second, the faint outline of her body right in front of me. Why the hell not? My clothes trailed across the concrete and Enola Gay had already eased into the water, a gentle ripple lapping the sides of the pool.

"Quiet now," she said.

I made out her breast tan lines as she leaned her arms on the pool edge. "Is it cold?"

"It feels great."

She offered her hand and I slid into the water. I entered an aquatic world and swam with hushed strokes, diving deep to the bottom, coming up for air, feeling bubbles spring to the surface. The sound underwater came alive with whooshes and gurgles. We cavorted like two dolphins playing in the wake of a boat.

We climbed out and lay side by side on the still-warm concrete, basking in its heat settling in my core. I reached over to Enola Gay, touching her shoulder.

"Ssshhh." She turned toward me and put her finger to my lips.

I half-rolled on top of Enola Gay and kissed her softly. She was an equal party to our exploration and our vibe gathered force. Breathing in short gasps, the hardness of her nipples rubbed against me. With the adroitness of a wrestler, she flipped me on my back, grasping between my legs.

She whispered, "Don't worry, it's a good time of the month."

I was inside her and she rocked on top of me with a fury until her back arched, a hushed moan rose, and I felt her quiver. A flare gun fired off in my loins and in a dazed sex-stupor, I realized, so this is what all the fuss is about.

Her crying was quiet at first and built to sobbing, causing her whole body to shudder as she lay on top of me, knees drawn up. Tears trickled down my neck, leaving warms tracks across my shoulders. I put my arms around Enola Gay and felt her inner turmoil right through her rib cage. I didn't understand any of it at first. Was she mad at me? Was I that bad at sex? It came to me—she was angry—not at me, but at the world, at her father, at life. I never knew so much pain and anguish, couldn't fathom it until now. It burned her to the core and the flames licked me. The anger I felt at her father and the destruction he rained down on his family singed everyone, including the innocent bystanders. I can't say I blamed her. No friends, a broken family, starting over. It was scary to contemplate and as I stared past her into the endless murk of the solar system, I wondered how I'd do in the same situation. I only wanted to let her cling to me. I was only a kid, but deep down I sensed I was going to be scarred by this in my own way.

The call we knew was coming arrived a week after our poolside tryst. Enola Gay dragged the phone and extension line into her bedroom while she talked to her mom. Hanging up, she walked into the living room with the phone in her hand as if it was some unwanted appendage. "I'm going home. To Texas." Although I knew she wanted to see her mom, she didn't look happy, her expression stuck in neutral. After three months with us, she was comfortable sticking her neck out of her shell.

Our goodbyes at the Philadelphia Airport were filled with hugs and wet eyes. Enola Gay took off and the jet veered west until it disappeared into a red ball of sun. We promised to call and write, and we did—for a while, but time and distance are twins, and I couldn't tell if they soothed or numbed. Their toll, after a few months, meant only a sporadic letter, shorter each time, arriving in the mail. It was like hollering into a long tunnel, sound reverberating, murmuring, until there was no sound at all.

* * *

The years went by, then decades. College. First job. Marriage. Kids. Too busy or distracted to keep up with anything but putting one foot forward at a time. I lost track of all the Little League practices, school conferences, and PTA meetings I attended.

It was all a blur. One minute I was sitting at the top of the bleachers, then I dropped off a cliff when my wife passed away from ovarian cancer three years ago. I was drained and untethered. In the garage, my electronic parts and circuit boards gathered dust while the soldering guns hung, unused, on the metal mounts in the peg board above the work bench.

On a business trip to Cleveland, I browsed the Hudson's book store in the airport, killing time before my flight back to Philadelphia. The newspaper headlines were filled with President Trump cozying up to the nuclear despot, "Rocket Man" Kim Jong Un, and terminating missile treaties with Russia. A table, with books arranged like tiles, was out front and I picked among them.

I don't remember the title of the book but the author's name brought a flood of memories: Enola Gay. I opened the dust jacket and turned to the back flap. There she was, sitting at a desk in a thoughtful authorial pose with a wall of books behind her. The liner notes mentioned she was a professor of literature at the University of Texas. She'd done it. Enola Gay was scarred but she was a survivor. Not everyone was so lucky. She had risen from the ashes of her childhood.

As I looked at the gray-haired woman in the picture with a still-indecipherable smile, I remembered our friendship during a small pane in the window of life. I let out an audible chuckle and the woman next to me at Hudson's shifted down the aisle. Enola Gay had a rebirth, and I believed I could do the same.

Turning to the back cover, I noticed I could 'follow' Enola Gay on Facebook so I pulled my iPhone out of my pocket and opened the Facebook search function. Finding her, I stared at the minimal profile she shared unless you were a friend. I expected nothing less from her.

I decided to climb back to that window and hope it was open. I pushed the Facebook 'Friend' button, feeling my life was going to change in a dramatic way.

ACKNOWLEDGMENTS

Grateful acknowledgment is extended to the following publications in which these stories previously appeared:

"The Lookout" – *Woven Tale Press*

"Greyhound Cowboy" – *Clackamas Literary Review*

"Fall, Buck, and Scale" – *The Account*

"The Last Scrabble Game at Beaver Swamp" – *Cowboy Jamboree*

"Walking Out" – *Cirque*

"Ned Thayer – Outdoorsman" – *Adelaide Magazine*

"Palm Sunday" – *Entropy*

"The Distance Between Two Points" – *Poor Yorick Journal*

"Into the Black" – *Red Rock Review*

"Ashes" – *Kansas City Voices*

"Enola Gay" – *Red Fez*

Special thanks to my wife, Anne; the Juneau Writing Group; Evan Morgan Williams; Scott Pedersen; the staff at Cornerstone Press (Dr. Ross Tangedal, Brett Hill, Ellie Atkinson, Ava Willett, Sophie McPherson); and all the others who provided support and encouragement.

KEN POST, originally from the suburbs of New Jersey, retired from the Forest Service after working in Alaska for forty years. His fiction has appeared in *Clackamas Literary Review, Entropy, Red Rock Review, Cirque,* and others. He has been nominated for two Pushcart Prizes. He lives in Juneau, Alaska.